How to Date a Nerd

CASSIE MAE

COOKIE
Lynn

Also by Cassie Mae

Young Adult

Reasons I Fell for the Funny Fat Friend

Friday Night Alibi

Secret Catch

You Can't Catch Me

YA Series

How to Date a Nerd

How to Seduce a Band Geek

How to Hook a Bookworm

King Sized Beds and Happy Trails

Beach Side Beds and Sandy Paths

Lonesome Beds and Bumpy Roads

True Love and Magic Tricks

New Adult

Switched

The Real Thing

Unexpectedly You

Adult Series

Doing It for Love

No Interest in Love

Crazy About Love

Dedicated to anyone who's had a hard time embracing

how awesome they are.

Chapter 1

If I say I'm sick, don't kiss me!

Rules of keeping up your popular rep:

Number one, the shorter the skirt, the better.

Number two, natural hair color is a thing of the past.

Number three, high heels are an extension of your foot. To go without them would be like losing a toe.

Number four, guys are disposable, and should never be used more than once or for an extended period of time.

And number five, never *ever* reveal you collect Star Wars memorabilia, you know every line to Lord of the Rings, and you actually know the birthdates of all the Harry Potter cast members.

Yeah. I'm a total closeted nerd.

I'm not cool with pity glares in the hallways, painful jabs, and social scars. No thanks. It's much easier to keep my true nature hidden beneath layers of eyeliner, skimpy outfits, and even I must admit to myself, a rockin' body. Though the pushup bras tend to do most of the work.

Welcome to high school. Where everyone tries to be someone else.

Well… everyone except Zak.

Here's the DL on my next door neighbor. He's labeled King Dork because he wears nerdy shirts and talks in geek code. His front pocket of the plaid overshirt he wears always has at least three or four Pokémon cards in it. And if it's not that then it's a graphing calculator he has to keep shoving down so it doesn't fall out. There's a Star Wars keychain always clipped to the back of his holey jeans and he sometimes carries a Wii controller in his back pocket.

And I've got it bad for the boy.

It's not just the fact he was the one to introduce me to the awesomeness of the Elvish Language, the hidden mysteries of World of Warcraft, and the magical world that lies beyond Platform 9 ¾, but really, he pulls off sexy geek so damn well! His dark, like super dark eyes and his matching hair that flops around his forehead when he's laughing too hard, combined with his nice height, swoon… he's like the Peter Parker of my high school.

I may be the only person who finds his nerdiness so hecka irresistible. Everyone else treats him like some dead bug on the sidewalk. I know how it is, and I have no idea how he handles all the verbal abuse.

Middle school Zoe—Geek Zoe, I like to call her—was made fun of and tormented so much she spent most nights crying into her pillow. High school was the break I was totally looking for. A chance to freaking rewrite myself into someone who's socially acceptable. Summer before school started, I grabbed loads of magazines and watched all those teen movies that so aren't as awesome as Star Trek, but they were for my status education. And apparently, I was doing this popularity thing all wrong. I gotta be like a major bitch to people, and I'll end up getting the hottest guy in the end.

Took some work, but I think I got it down. I should win an Oscar with how awesome I am at the fake personality.

But freak, it's been two years since I was de-geek-a-fied, and I still find myself trying to stifle the urge to buy Comic-Con tickets, and try not to act jealous when I see Zak dressing up for the event.

Don't get me wrong, my life is pretty darn fantastic and a whole heap lot better than the alternative, which is getting my emotional butt kicked around. So the fake persona is definitely worth it.

There's a huge party tonight. Lots of alcohol and boys, but like every party night, I try to show off first to my neighbor, who can see straight into my open window.

I strip down to my underwear so Zak can get a good look and turn up the music on my iPod. If he sneaks a peek, I can always throw my hands up and be like, "Whoops! I'm changing with the window open again, aren't I? So sorry." Then make a nice sexy show of closing the curtains. It looks perfect in my head, even though it's completely pathetic I have to resort to *this*. I'm trying way too hard to get his attention, but I don't care. It's not like I can flirt with him at school. Social suicide bomb right there.

Stealing glances out my window into his, I flaunt around my room pretending like I'm getting ready for the party. But I can't get a good view of him, and I don't want to be more obvious than I already am.

Nothing.

Huh, maybe he's not...

Yikes! I've reached my LOST playlist and my heart stumbles over itself as I quickly turn the music back down until I can get a more trendy song on.

"Hey, I was listening to that," a voice says from outside my window. I *knew* he was home. Darn boy ignoring a prancing half-naked girl next door. Gosh, I thought I was doing this right. I adjust my bra to make my boobs look extra luscious, and then smoothly appear in his line of sight.

Zak is at his computer, books piled next to him. He rubs his eyes and blinks a couple times before staring back at the screen, brow furrowed. Totally not looking at me or my boobs.

"What exactly were you listening to?" I ask, using my seductive voice guys, well, *most* guys fall over.

Looking at me—about time—he shakes his head at my revealing attire before reaching over to a cord I can't see. His blinds shut with a rejected *smack!*

Youch.

I examine my boobs, but there's nothing wrong there. Maybe I have a booger or something.

Nope. No booger, no drool, nothing.

Just me.

Great, now I'm all self-conscious. What's wrong with me? I turn around in circles trying to examine my butt, but all I can think is I miss my Star Wars panties. These lacey ones are okay, Popular Zoe 101, but there's nothing cooler than having a big Storm Trooper head slapped across my butt cheeks. Well, if I can't even impress my nerdboy, I'm not going to even attempt a party appearance.

I throw on my pajamas—the big unflattering ones—and slouch on the bed. Stupid geek boy and the hold he has on me. I shouldn't care what he thinks.

But I do. Because I care what *everybody* thinks.

I sigh and look out the window again. The sun dips below the horizon casting orange and yellow streaks across Zak's blinds, like something out of Harry Potter. Just super full of cool magic beans. I wonder if Zak's still sitting there at his computer, typing away or plunging his nose into one of his thousands of books.

I shake my head. What does it matter what he's doing? I. Should. Not. Care.

I hop off the bed, slam my own blinds shut and whip the curtains together. My gaze flicks to the shelves lining the wall. They have been carefully constructed to conceal accusing material, with colorful doors that slide across it, revealing some things, and hiding others. Out of habit, I check over my shoulder before I slide open one of the doors, hiding the lines of lip-gloss and compact mirrors and opening the section of the shelf holding several books about the X-Men.

I quickly grab the desired book and a flashlight and slam the door shut. Some of the lip-gloss topples over, but I make no attempt to straighten them. Must get under the covers stat! I curl up in the middle of my bed and throw the comforter over myself.

My sanctuary lies here as I open the book I've read thousands of times and purge my mind with paragraphs about Dark Phoenix. Jean Grey is my idol. No one will ever know, but I base most of my wardrobe off her.

I don't know how long it's been before my phone buzzes on my nightstand. Yeah, my mind turns off to the rest of the world when I nerd-out. I turn off the flashlight and pull the comforter off my head, keeping the book hidden as I reach over for the cell.

My stomach used to flutter whenever I read Cody's name on the caller I.D. but now I feel nothing. I really don't want to talk to my current boyfriend. He'd call me some absurd pet name and ask where I was. So I let voicemail grab it.

I hear the text jingle a few minutes later as I am carefully placing my book back on its shelf.

Where is ur sxy ass???? U better get here b4 any more chicks hit on me.

Ugh. I think his ego can keep him company for a while. Still, I let him know who's in charge of this relationship.

Another rule that's off the record: stay in control of all the boys you let kiss you. That way they don't end up in your pants unless you want them there.

I'm sick. Thx so much 4 ur concern.

There's no response, but I don't care. It won't be the first boyfriend who found someone new before breaking it off with me. I do *not* put out. Though, I don't care if they tell people I do. Helps with the rep without me actually having to do that part with guys who've been with who knows who. Score!

I kinda feel bad for the girl who ends up in his arms tonight. Cody is a totally status thing. I use him and he uses me. We both know it, and neither of us really cares. It's been about three weeks, so we've pretty much hit our limit anyway. He is a good kisser though.

I'll give him that one.

I look at the closed curtains, thinking of another boy with amazing kissing abilities, but I shove the thought from my mind before I lose it completely to blissed out Zak happyland.

"Hey, I thought you were going out tonight?" My younger sister waltzes in and plops on my bed. Her dark brown hair has been curled into corkscrews, and she's covered in pounds of makeup. She's wearing a blue shirtdress with a thick belt around her middle, making what little bosom she has look bigger. She's only fourteen, but in this outfit, and that hair, she could pass for my age. I raise my eyebrows at her.

"And you thought you'd tag along?"

"Mom and Dad won't know, and I'll leave you alone. I promise."

I shake my head. "I'm not going. So you can't either."

"Why not?"

"There's gonna be alcohol, Sierra."

She gives me a look that says "You're the biggest hypocrite." She's totally right so I play the tattletale card.

"And because I'll tell Mom and Dad you went out while they were gone."

She stands and smiles. "You know, if you're going to start tossing around threats, I'd be a little more worried about what *I'd* tell them about *you*."

I give her my best impression of Gollum on crack. "Fine, go out. See if they even let you in without me."

She tosses her hair over her shoulder and narrows her eyes.

"Fine. I will." She storms out of my room, and my gut tells me to go after her, but my pride blocks my exit.

I sit and catch my breath before I finally get out into the hallway.

"Sierra, wait!" I call down the stairs. Hopefully I've caught her in time. Letting my fourteen-year-old sister go to an all-night alcohol fountain party wouldn't exactly make me a responsible older sister, even though I never really fit into that category. Still seems wrong to at least not try to get her to stay.

"Sierra!" I get to the bottom of the staircase, and she comes out from the formal living room scaring the crap out of me.

"Someone's here to see you," she says bitterly as she pushes me to the side to get upstairs. Instead of socking her in the butt, like I want to, I kink my neck to see around the wall. What the hell is Cody doing here? His back is turned to me, and he's holding something in his hand. I duck back upstairs to change into my sexy pajamas. No way is he seeing me in these old baggy ones.

I grab the black silk shorts and cami and slip them on. I let my fake deep red hair down—you know, Jean Grey— so it cascades down my back, and I quickly run my fingers through it. I don't worry about makeup, just slab some gloss on my lips. After all, I am 'sick'. But girls like me have to look good at their worst.

I throw a light blanket over my shoulders and walk back to Cody. He still has his back to the entryway.

Okay Geek Zoe, it's been fun, but Cody can't know you exist.

I take another deep breath and get ready for my act. "What are you doing here?" I ask, letting my phony anger soak into my voice.

He turns around, and his eyes widen at my ensemble.

See? There's nothing wrong with *me*. It's Zak who has a problem.

"Uh…" he stutters as he clears his head. "I thought maybe since you were too sick to go out, we'd stay in." He holds up a movie, which I'm surprised to see is a total chick flick. Gross. But popular Zoe likes that crap.

"Do you feel guilty about something?" I've been through this stuff before. He's totally trying to make up for something he did that he shouldn't have done.

Oh well, time for a new boyfriend anyway.

His eyes lower to the floor, and I take in a deep breath and wait for it. The inevitable "I cheated on you" or "I found someone else."

"I'm sorry about that text. I didn't mean to make you upset. I was only kidding, really."

I stare at him, not able to erase the shock from my face. "Huh?"

"I know you haven't had the best luck when it came to your ex's. I was being stupid. Forgive me?" He tosses me a puppy dog face.

Now I'm really thrown and I'm not sure how to respond. So I just mumble incoherencies.

"Um… I guess… sure… uh-huh…"

"So," he says furrowing his brow and crossing over to me, "we're cool?"

I give him a nod, but then remember I have a part to play. I fold my arms across my waist and gaze up into his handsome face. His dark hair has been tousled across his forehead and frames his deep brown eyes perfectly. He's getting five o'clock shadow on his cheeks and chin. Yeah… definitely a status thing with him.

"Don't treat me like that. I deserve better." I don't really mean that. In fact, right now I deserve a lot worse.

"I promise it won't happen again."

He takes me into his arms, but I keep mine folded, not responding to his hug. I do let out a fake sigh of defeat and say into his chest, "Okay."

He pulls back and tilts my face to slap a kiss on me. As usual, I remove myself from the embrace—metaphorically—and think about more pleasant company. Maybe Obi-Wan, but not like old fart Obi-Wan. Heck, I'd take Neville Longbottom before I made-out with an old guy, even if he did have The Force. Though, Neville's gotten pretty hot over the years. Guess we all have to go through the awkward phase. Except Zak. He's always been hot. Graphing calculator and all.

Right when I'm about to imagine another awesome kissing candidate, a different kind of urgency pushes from behind Cody's lips, and I'm snapped back into reality. I pull away, afraid of what he's thinking.

"I'm sick, remember," I say wiping my soggy lips with the tips of my fingers. Gag.

"I don't care," he says as he tries to pull me in again. I put my hands on his chest and push back, leaning my head away from his face.

"I do." I use my stern and controlling voice, but it's not fake this time. He better keep those pervy lips away from me.

He looks like he wants to argue, but he lets go. I almost let out the huge sigh of relief I'd been holding in my chest, but I catch it before I do. I mean, for all he knows, I'm a girl who lets just about anyone between her legs. He entwines his fingers with mine and mumbles, "So... do you want me to go?"

"Yeah. I don't want you to catch it."

"You don't sound sick." His voice is barely audible.

"Well, I am."

He pauses a moment and looks behind me, into the hallway. I crane my neck to see what he's looking at, but I'm forced back into an awkward embrace, his mouth trying to swallow me whole.

I can't move. His fingers latch onto my upper back and yank some of my hair. *What the hell is he doing?* I start clawing at his body, trying to break free from his strong arms.

"Holy shit, Cody!" I shout the second I get his face away from me. "What the hell was that?"

"Come on, Zoe." His hands continue to dig into my back. I wish I would've kept the baggy pajamas on because I'm sure he's drawing blood.

"Get. Off. Me." I'm wiggling around, hoping he'll let me go, but his grip tightens.

He smiles. Not one that's sexy or anything, but a very nasty and uber creepy grin. If my legs weren't trapped, I'd knee him right in the balls. "Every guy you've been with only dated you to get in your pants." His grip tightens again, and I try to keep my face as far away from his as I can. "You know it. I know it. You can't be mad at me for doing exactly what you were doing."

"Which is what?" I spit. He really needs to let go before I go batshit crazy on him. This is getting really scary.

"Dating each other till we got something out of it."

My eyes fill up, and the tears almost spill over. He's right. Which sucks. I'm so stupid. I should have expected at least one of the boys I dated to be upset about not getting some, so upset they'd take it into their own hands.

"I want you to leave me alone."

"I helped you out. How many people get jealous whenever I touch you?" He reaches up and brushes my hair from my face. I'm tempted to bite his finger off. "How many clubs have you gotten into because I know someone?" His lips are near inches away from mine, his hand now locked around my jaw so I can't move. "I think since I've done my part, it's only fair you do yours."

My lips form obscenities around his as he mashes them against me. I'm wiggling like crazy, trying with every bit of strength I have to get away from him. I think I got in a good hit somewhere, but he's not letting go.

He bites down on my bottom lip, causing a yelp of pain to escape my mouth. I keep quiet after that, and he moves his kisses to my cheeks, my neck, my chest, while I still try to get out of his grasp.

Is this really happening? What is he going to do to me? How far will this go? I try to detach myself—again metaphorically—but it's impossible. No one has ever attacked me like this before, and tears start to leak out the corners of my eyes.

One of his hands clasps my butt cheek as he moves me upstairs. My stomach plummets as I hope against all hope Sierra stays in her room. She can *not* see this. I don't want her to see this.

We get to the top of the landing, and I hear a doorknob turn, but it's not from Sierra's room. It's the front door which is in plain view from where Cody has me pinned. Cody hears it too and he shoots upright, letting go of me long enough so I can fix my top before someone walks in.

"Hello?"

I'm too relieved to be confused about Zak standing in the doorway. I jog down the stairs, coming within inches of his body, but stop myself from hugging him. My arms drop, and I pretend I was going to scratch my head, looking like an idiot. His puzzled face would be comical if it weren't for the tense atmosphere. I take a small step away as Cody descends the staircase. I search deep inside my voice box for a cheery tone and blink away the water from my eyes. "Hey, uh… my dad'll be home in a minute and he can get you that book you wanted. I'm not sure where he put it. You can sit over there if you wanna wait."

I'm so glad Zak knows when to act stupid and when to play along. "Thanks, Zoe." He goes into the living room and sits down, not taking his eyes off me and my now *very* ex-boyfriend. No way will that guy ever get near me again. Cody looks like he got attacked by fire ants with how red he is. He clears his throat and looks at me.

"I better get back to the party. You coming?"

"No." Hell no. I don't look him in the eyes, because now they scare the crap out of me. "I'm sick remember."

"Your loss." He shrugs out the front door, and I almost break into tears right there in the entryway. But Zak's presence shuts me off from losing it.

"Are you all right?" he asks getting off the couch and stepping closer to me. I quickly try to erase the pain and horror from my face, putting my calm mask on.

"Yeah. I'm not feeling well, like I told Cody. So, I'm going to go upstairs and sleep it off."

"Zoe, don't pretend like I don't know what just happened."

I feel all the color drain from my body. So much for looking calm. "What do you mean?"

Zak bores his eyes into mine. I fold my arms again and stare back. He's not going to get me to admit to anything. I'm not even sure what happened. It's like my mind can't catch up with the reality of it all.

"Well, next time I see him attack you like that, I'm calling the cops."

A hard lump drops in my tummy, and I gaze out the window behind him, to the perfect view of his kitchen. I know how that kiss—or attack—felt from here, but how did it look from there?

"It's nothing to worry about," I lie. "Really, it's always like that." Now I give him a fake smile, trying to push back my embarrassment and fear.

"If that's the case, I'm calling the cops right now."

"Wait," I say coming up short on excuses. I don't know why I care so much, or why I'm giving Zak the attitude, especially since he just saved me from something I never would've thought… I mean, Cody could've… ugh, I can't think about it anymore. I'm getting more and more panicked, and I want up in my room, under my blankets so I can curl up with Wolverine and not think about what just happened. And even though Zak did something for me I can't even think of how to repay him for, I find myself trying to keep up my fake persona. "Don't call the cops. I… uh… we got in a fight, and he wanted to make up. And… uh, I wasn't exactly done being mad at him, you know?" Great now I sound like a rambling fool.

Zak studies my face. His eyes search mine for any deception, but since what I said isn't completely untrue, he lets it go.

"Okay. Sorry I barged in. I thought it was a problem."

"No, there's no problem." I try to smile. "Promise."

He studies my face once again before going out the door. I hadn't realized I'd been holding my breath until the hot air escapes my nose. I jog upstairs, slam my bedroom door and put on my baggy pajamas before curling up under my sheets and crying myself to sleep.

Chapter 2

Why couldn't I have been an only child?

I wake up Monday morning filled with panic and anxiety. I don't want to see Cody, or act like everything is okay after what happened last Friday. I don't feel like acting at all, but since I've already skipped so many classes, one more and I'll be kicked out, so I sit in front of the mirror and prepare my mask for the day.

I can see Zak from my window again. He's already dressed and shoving a large book into his bag. He's wearing a blue plaid button-up shirt over his "Use the Force" T-shirt. I can't believe he wears that stuff to school, even if he does look pretty great in it, I'm probably one out of two people who think that. His dark brown hair falls right above his ears, so part of it covers his eyes as I try to get his attention by coughing or sighing loudly.

He doesn't acknowledge me at all, which I try to seem fine with. I don't know why I want his attention so badly. He's made it pretty clear he doesn't see me that way, and I don't blame him after what I did. I may swoon and sway as I look at him from across our windows, but in school, if I even glanced in his direction, I'd get shit for it.

I turn back to the mirror and let out a sigh—a real one this time. The dark circles under my eyes make it look like I've been on drugs for the past few days, when really, I've just been up every hour reliving those few scary seconds in Cody's unrelenting grasp. My long fake red hair is matted and knotty from not brushing it after my shower last night. Do I have my work cut out for me this morning or what?

I plug in the flat iron and get up to dig through my closet. If I'm going to convince people I'm okay, I need something short and sexy, pushing the boundaries of the dress code. I slip on a tight miniskirt and a low-cut pink top and assess the outfit. Besides the horror that is my face and hair, I look pretty damn hot. Just like the girls in those movies. We're on the right track, baby!

My hair takes me a good twenty minutes to untangle, and I slather globs of makeup to cover my raccoon eyes. Perfect, and just in time, too. First period starts in fifteen minutes. I throw my purse over my shoulder—only losers wear backpacks—tuck my Algebra II book under my arm and head out the door.

My car isn't in the driveway, though. Great, this shit of a morning keeps getting better and better. Even though I know it's really childish, I stomp my foot on the cement.

Sierra!

I could strangle her until her brain starts working. It had to be her. It isn't the first time she's stolen my car to ditch school. Being underage doesn't stop her from swiping my keys the second my parents leave for work.

And now I'm going to be really late. I kick off my heels and curl the straps around my fingers as I walk barefoot down the sidewalk. Just when I think my day couldn't get much worse, I feel a light splash on my arm. How cliché. I pick up the pace as the rain starts to fall and fold my body around my book to keep it from getting wet. So much for taking time to do my hair. Oh, I'm going to kill Sierra!

A shiver runs up my spine, and I'm instantly regretting the short and slinky outfit. I'd take wearing my own "Use the Force" shirt over freezing to death. I consider turning back and staying home for the day, but the possibility of getting expelled propels me forward.

Why can't I graduate without actually *going* to school?

I start running. The balls of my feet smack the pavement, and I pray I don't end up stepping on anything that would cause serious damage. Rain water splashes up my legs as I run through the puddles. If I slip and fall, that's it for my morning.

The glow of headlights flickers behind me. Maybe some fool will take pity on me and give me a ride to school.

"Zoe?"

His voice always sends a wave of butterflies through my stomach, and I can't help the dorky grin that forms on my face.

"Yeah, it's me!" I call back over the weather.

"Get in!"

He doesn't need to tell me twice.

"Thanks," I say once I'm in.

"No problem." Zak puts the truck in first gear and eases back onto the road. Driving stick adds the sexy to this wonderful geekboy.

"Feeling better, I see." He smirks out of the side of his mouth, and I roll my eyes.

"Shut up." I wring out my hair on the leather seat and give him a fake grimace. He laughs as he wipes it up with one of the plaid overshirts he keeps in the cab.

We don't talk for a few seconds while Zak messes around with the radio. How he does that and drive a manual, I have no idea.

"You know, there's a new Spiderman documentary on this weekend."

No freakin' way! How did I not know about this? My heart jumps through a hoop of excitement, but I keep my face composed. "So?"

"Maybe we could watch it together. Just like old times."

Is he for real? My dorky grin almost comes back, but I keep it restrained.

He steals a glance at me and says quickly, "It'll be a bunch of us. Ariana's coming, I think."

I want to go—oh boy, do I want to—and if it was just going to be the two of us, I probably would say, "Heck yes!" But it's not, and that's social suicide. If I'm going to watch it…scratch that, *when* I watch it, I'll do it hidden in my room with the curtains drawn and the door securely locked.

I force an amused "as if" chuckle and gaze at the raindrops slipping down the window.

"Well, you'll miss out. Stan Lee is hosting it."

"Who?" My voice drizzles with sarcasm, and he lets out a booming laugh.

"All right. I won't bug you about it."

He shifts gears again, and I see the muscles on his forearm

ripple. When did he get those? He certainly didn't have them when…ah, never mind.

My phone buzzes between my cleavage. I pull it out, trying to emphasize the fact I'm touching my boobs, but Zak focuses on the road in front of us. His indifference makes my face heat as I slide the phone open.

I need ur help! I'm about a block away from Kevin's house. Plz hurry.

Sierra. What has she gotten into now? Even though I'm pissed at her, I suppose I should at least answer her urgent message. I fill my cheeks with air and let it come out slowly as my fingers fly across my keyboard.

I can't. I'm gonna B late for school. Call Mom or Dad.

"You okay?" Zak looks at my face, which is still half blown up.

"Yeah."

"You sure? You always do that when you're frustrated."

I narrow my eyes. "Do what?"

"Hold your breath." His dark eyes shine with amusement, and I wish I was in the mood to appreciate that he still remembers things like that about me. Blowing up my cheeks always helped with the anxiety when I was called names in middle school.

"I'm fine."

My phone buzzes again.

I can't. Please! They'll kill me if they knew I ditched school. I need you Zoe.

Argh! Curse my sisterly nature. Zak is about to pull into the school parking lot, but maybe he won't mind being late.

"Zo?"

Oh, I love it when Zak calls me that.

"Yeah?"

He pulls into the parking lot and shuts off the truck. When he takes his hand off the gear shift thingy, he rubs the sweat from his palm on his jeans. "You sure everything is okay?" He keeps his eyes locked on his knees. "'Cause you don't look okay."

Apparently, I'm transparent. "Could you take me somewhere else? My sister needs help with something."

He cocks an eyebrow at me. Man, I wish I could do that without looking like a complete dork.

"Don't you have enough tardies?"

"Yeah, but it sounds like she's in trouble."

Zak nods and starts the car, but instead of heading out of the parking lot, he pulls up to the school doors. I open my mouth to snap at him, but his concerned face stops me.

"You go to class. I'll get Sierra."

"But—"

"Don't argue with me, Zoe. I can afford to be late, but you can't. I don't want to see you get kicked out because your sister ditched to see her boyfriend."

"How did you…?"

"It's not hard to guess."

I want to kiss him. Yeah, I totally want to smack one right there on his nerdy lips. I want to wrap my arms around him and let him know how much I appreciate his concern, because I don't deserve those worry lines he's got on his forehead.

Okay, so I lied. He's nothing like Peter Parker. He's a bajillion times sexier than Peter Parker. Spiderman ain't got nothing on Zak Gibbons.

But we're right in front of school. It's bad enough I'm in the truck with him. To be seen kissing King Dork? I may as well wear my Harry Potter shirt to class.

So I mutter thank you, tell him the address Sierra just sent, and get out of the truck before anyone can see.

School really isn't so bad. Class is my favorite part. I like learning new crap, especially if I connect it to *Star Wars* or *Lord of the Rings*. But I fail most of my tests on purpose. Not enough to fail the class, but to eke by without being called an egghead or a moron.

I make it to first period right as the bell rings. Ms. Weber isn't even here yet. I take my seat in the back, where I'm usually surrounded by my self-righteous friends, but they're all late today.

"Hey, Zoe." Hannah waves at me, and I try to cock my eyebrow like Zak does, but I'm sure I look ridiculous. To cover, I give a demeaning little wave back. Hannah is not in my social circle. My brief acknowledgment causes her face to flush. I fight the urge to care about it. That Zoe can't exist at school.

"Turn your phones off now unless you want me to chuck them against the wall," Ms. Weber says as she finally walks in. She's wearing a tight mauve dress, and her blonde hair is done up in an elegant braid. Her red lipstick and perfectly formed cheekbones make her face look flawless. Needless to say, she's the hot teacher all the boys drool over.

My phone is tucked safely between my boobs, and Zak's not in this class so I don't pull it out to turn it off. He probably wouldn't look anyway.

Ms. Weber dives into her lesson about Ancient Egypt, and I find myself leaning forward, enthralled with the information, but trying to keep my face nonchalant. Halfway through the lecture, Zak walks in like he's just run a freaking marathon.

"Mr. Gibbons," Ms. Weber says, folding her arms over her waist. "I believe you are in my fifth period class. You're a tad early."

Giggles float through the air, but Zak takes no notice of them.

"Sorry to interrupt, but they need Zoe in the main office."

Ms. Weber turns her back on him and continues to write on the whiteboard. Zak waves me over. I take Ms. Weber's lack of response as an okay and grab my purse.

Someone wolf whistles, and I throw the bird out behind my back and laugh, trying to play it light so they don't think I'm enjoying company with Lord of the Nerds, even though inches from his cologne makes me drool like a darn puppy dog. A loud "Oooh," echoes around the room. People are so stupid, but I'm glad Zak doesn't grab my arm to pull me into the hallway. More whistles would have ensued, and I can only do so much here.

I'm pretty sure I'm the only one who looks past his nerdy shirts and personality. Or thinks that adds to his cuteness level while everyone else writes him off. But Zak and I…we used to be stitched together in middle school. The two geeks who spoke Elvish and played Pokémon in the band pit. Gah! It took *forever* to rid myself of that reputation. Sure, it was fun and stuff, but I was never invited to the cool parties or asked out, like…ever.

Totally changed now, thank you very much. But I still have major anxiety attacks when I think about the stuff people said behind my back. To my face, too, I guess. Zak kind of held me together back then. Every time I'd have an "episode," he'd pull me into the janitor closet—not for "seven minutes in heaven," that's so not what happened—and rub my shoulders till my breathing calmed, and make me recite the different shortcuts in various video games. Totally took my mind off all the nasty stuff people called me, and got rid of the tears, too. Zak was awesome like that. Always seemed to be there when I needed him.

I still don't get what's wrong with him, though. I mean, didn't it hurt him, too? All the stuff people said about how dorky and loserish we were? Because it hurt me. It hurt a lot. He doesn't seem to care. I *wish* I could not care, but it's not possible. People want to *be* me now. Well, fake me. This is much better than crying over what people say about my Yoda backpack.

Then I think about Cody and wonder if it really is better, but shove the thought from my brain before I revert to Geek Zoe.

"What is it? Is Sierra okay?"

Zak shakes his head. "I got there just as the ambulance arrived."

My heart drops into my butt. "What?"

"She totaled your car, Zo. I'll take you to the hospital. Don't worry, she didn't look too bad when I saw her."

"I've gotta call my mom," I say, yanking out my phone. I don't care that this time he isn't looking at me.

"Come on," he says, pulling my arm. "You can call her on the way."

I nod and wiggle out of his hold.

I never knew Zak was capable of driving over the speed limit, but we could hydroplane with how fast he zooms through the neighborhood.

"Are you sure she's all right?" I ask as I cling to the seat for dear life.

"Yeah," he says, but he's short with me. Guess I shouldn't talk to him right now.

We get to the hospital and Zak drops me off right at the ER doors. As I'm clicking the seat belt, he clears his throat awkwardly. "Uh…I hope everything's okay."

"You're not staying?" The words are out of my mouth before I can stop them. I need him to stay. I should tell him thanks for the ride and let him go, but I can't. I need him in case Sierra—

"Only if you want me to."

He's giving me another chance to tell him to leave. I search myself for that fake persona, but I'm too panicked over my sister to act on it.

"Just go park the car. I'll need a ride home." That should be an okay response. I fly out of the truck before I can make more of a fool of myself.

The ER smells like death. I know that's a horrid thought when walking into a hospital, but I can't help it. A woman pukes in a bucket in the corner, a little boy holds his arm, which is bent at an awkward angle, and there's a man who is so drunk he can't hold his head up straight. Dude, it's nine in the morning!

The man behind the desk is organizing charts. When I get to him, I can already tell his Monday morning is way busier than he wants it to be.

"Put your name on the list. We'll be with you in a minute."

"I'm here to see my sister. She came in with the ambulance."

"What's her name?"

"Sierra."

His eyes finally flick to look me up and down. He raises his eyebrows at my wet outfit, and his face flushes. "Um, she's in room one-thirteen. I'll take you to her."

I'm used to guys falling over me, but I'm not in the mood to appreciate it. The receptionist or nurse whoever he is leads me through the back doors and down the smelly hallway. When we get to room one-thirteen, my heart is pumping in my throat.

Sierra has a few tubes sticking in her arms. Her head is bandaged and she's got stitches on her left cheek. She's silently crying as she stares at the picture hanging on the wall.

"Sierra."

She turns to look at me, and her silent tears grow into sloppy incoherencies. "Zoe, I-I don't know… I didn't mean… I really am sorry. Please… don't, don't tell… they would kill me."

Thank heavens for the sister translator. "I can't *not* say something. You won't be able to hide this."

"Please," she begs.

I shake my head and sit down next to her. I grab her hand, the one without the IV in it, and rub it. "Are you okay? What did the doctors tell you?"

"I'm fine. They have to scan my head or something 'cause I hit it so hard."

I suck in a steady breath through my nose. "You know, Mom and Dad probably already know about all of this."

She shoots me a dirty look. "You called them?"

"Yes, but they didn't answer. Sierra, you're in the hospital. They need, you know, insurance information, parental consent, that kind of stuff to treat you. And if you're getting an MRI, I'm almost positive Mom is on her way right now."

Her face gets twisted, and she yanks her arm from underneath my fingertips. "You suck Zoe! I thought you had my back and you go and call Mom."

"I do have your back. That's why I'm here."

"You don't! You called Mom when I told you not to!"

"What do you want me to do? They're going to find out about this. How stupid are you, Sierra?"

Tears stream from the corners of her eyes. She folds her arms and turns her face away.

"Leave me alone."

I shake my head and storm out of the room. I don't have to deal with this right now. Little brat didn't even appreciate I didn't yell at her for wrecking my car. If she doesn't want me here, fine, but she can't be alone. I swing the doors open to the ER lobby and find Zak standing awkwardly by the exit.

"Let's go," I say as I pass him.

He doesn't question it; he doesn't say anything at all. I whip my phone out and dial my mom's number again. She still doesn't answer, but I leave her a message.

"Hey Mom. Sierra's in the ER. She's in room one-thirteen and she seems okay, but I need to go back to school. Call me when you get this."

I ask Zak to wait in the hospital parking lot till I my mom calls. We don't have to wait long, but the few minutes of Zak rattling off things he hopes Stan Lee talks about on Friday—while I hold back all my geek knowledge—calms me down. Even after our falling out, my nerdy, sexy next door neighbor makes things better.

I wish I deserved it.

Chapter 3

I'm too tired to pretend today.

"Zoe! Get down here!"

An audible "ugh" escapes my lips. I know what's coming. The parade of questions.

What happened?

Why weren't you watching your sister?

Why didn't you wait at the hospital?

I really don't want to get into it, but better get this over with.

My dad is a large man. When I say large, I mean like six-foot-seven, and three-hundred plus pounds. The look on Cody's face was priceless when I introduced him.

Ugh. Let's not think about that perv right now.

Dad's leaning against the fridge, which has tilted off the ground slightly. His face is scrunched, and it looks like he's been holding his breath for the past few minutes. Mom is elbow high in soapy dish water. They're more upset than I thought. We have a dishwasher so Mom only hand washes when she's pissed about something. Or when she's really hurt.

And Dad only gets purple when Mom is hurt.

Crap.

"Care to tell us what happened this morning?" Dad's voice is calm, though his stance tells me he's trying to keep his anger in. Mom slops around in the sink.

"I don't know what happened," I say to the floor. "Sierra sent me this text and I didn't want to be late for class, so I thought if I sent Zak—"

"Gibbons?" My eyes click up to see my dad's furrowed brow. "You were skipping class with him?"

His confused expression slaps onto my face now. "Huh?"

He rubs his hand across his forehead. "Zoe, I won't tolerate being lied to. Give it to me straight please. Don't you care at all about what you did to your sister?"

"What?" My high-pitch screech was probably heard a hundred miles away. "What *I* did? I didn't do anything!"

"Don't lie to me!" I cower under his tone, and I know I'm about to go into hysterics. Dad, like, *never* yells.

Mom whimpers over the sink, and my dad stops leaning against the fridge. It slams against the floor as his weight leaves it. He curls his arms around Mom's waist.

I hate seeing her like this, and I *know* my dad hates seeing her like this, but I'm so confused I don't know what to say.

"Zoe." It's Mom's shattered voice that sends the tears cascading from my eyeballs. "I trust you to look after your sister, and you let her drive your car? What were you thinking?"

I feel the blood rise in my face. I'm probably as purple as my dad now. I ball my fists up and suck in a small wisp of air. *Sierra!*

"I *didn't* let her," I growl through my teeth. "She stole my car and took off before I even woke up. I had to get a ride with Zak today. You can check with him if you don't believe me."

My parents look at each other, eyes swapping questions. After a minute or two of this silent conversation, my dad snaps the phone off the wall. I hear Zak's house phone ring through the window.

"I need to speak with your boy, if that's okay Maddie." His voice is kind, but you can totally tell he's in a hurry.

I plop down on the bar stool and wait. Even though I know there shouldn't be anything to worry about since I'm telling the truth, my heart still whacks against my breastplate.

"Zak, this is Mr. Livingston… thank you, that's why I'm calling. Did Zoe go to school with you?" My dad's eyes burn into mine as he waits for Zak to answer. He's quiet for a while.

"Thank you. You've helped clear up the issue. Have a good night." Dad clicks the end button and stands frozen for a minute. Both me and Mom hold our breath.

Then without warning, Dad takes two long steps and wraps me into a hug. He never apologizes… never. So I'm not expecting him to say anything, but this is fine. I smile into his chest, and I can hear my mom fighting back more tears.

When I pull back, Mom takes Dad's place. "I'm sorry honey. Sierra told us differently."

Of course she did.

"It's okay, Mom. I'm sorry I didn't stay at the hospital with her. I… you know… school stuff."

She nods and pats me on the cheek. My dad still hasn't said anything, but that's just how he is.

* * *

Back in my room, I yank on my baggy pajamas. I'm really in no mood to be fake, or pretend. It's not like I have anyone to impress in my bedroom. And after what happened today, all I need is my X-Men book.

With flashlight in hand, I purge into the pages, wiping away stupid tears. I have no idea why I'm crying. Even though she stole my car, wrecked it, and then told my parents I was the one who did everything, I still can't help but feel guilty for leaving her in the hospital with tubes hanging out of her.

I'm a horrible sister.

I hear Zak's window slide open, and my stomach flutters.

Ugh! I hate the effect he still has on me.

I whip the comforter off my head, and my hair pops with all the static. Zak chuckles as he leans out his window. I quickly run my hand through my hair, turning red.

"Your sister get home okay?"

"Yeah." I crawl off the bed, trying to look sexy about it, but I'm not sure if I pull it off. I duck out my window so I can hear him better. Our property lines are so close, if we both extended our arms, we could hold hands.

"You're not in trouble are you?"

I shake my head, but drop my gaze to the bushes below us.

"What's wrong, Zo?"

I shake my head again, pursing my lips. No way am I confiding in him. That would send me down a very dangerous path resulting in a drop on the social ladder.

"Come on. We used to talk about everything."

I cringe. "I know."

"Didn't know you hated it so much."

I look up at him. His hair has fallen in front of his eyes, but I can see the hurt behind them.

"I didn't hate it. Things are just," I pause trying to find the right word. When he meets my stare, I finally find it. "Different."

He nods and chuckles. "I guess you could say that."

An awkward silence spreads between us. I blow up my cheeks but stop when I see Zak smirk at me. But then his smile fades, and his brow furrows.

"Zo, why…?" He doesn't finish, and I don't prod. I don't want to know what's going on in his head.

"Thanks for covering for me."

"I just told him the truth."

"Well, thanks."

Awkward silence again. He tosses his head back, sending his hair in a flurry. My stomach does a pancake flip as his dark eyes rest on mine. "I'll see you tomorrow."

He slams his window down and shuts the blinds.

I reciprocate, nearly breaking the glass.

On top of being a horrible sister, I'm a horrible neighbor.

My bed looks comfortable, but I plop down on the floor. I grab the edge of the comforter and wrap it around myself.

Stupid boy and all the jacked up feelings I get when I'm around him. He's a friggin' loser! He wore a Stars Wars shirt today. He invited me to watch a documentary this weekend. And the worst part is: *I'm* jealous of *him*.

I can't help but feel the same things I had when we were… friends. I suppose that's the best way to describe the relationship we had. But there are reasons why we aren't that way anymore. We're just so…

Different.

But that isn't his fault. It's mine.

I throw the comforter over my head and close my eyes to escape the pain growing in my chest.

I'm a horrible person. Period.

Chapter 4

I'm covering my mouth with duct tape next time

I'm at the salon.

Best way to cure self-inflicted pain? Go back to routine. Starting with the monthly trip to the hair salon with one of my popular buds, Hope.

"What's it gonna be this time, hon?" Missy totally has a hairstylist's name. I think it's a requirement for every student when they go through cosmetology school. If you don't have one, get one.

"Can we make it darker?"

"Darker red? Or black?"

"Red." Ahem... Jean Grey.

She nods and goes to prepare the dye. I run my fingers through the crispy strands. I used a cheap box last time and got a disproving look from Missy when she saw it. Gosh, it's not like I can poop out eighty bucks every month.

I mean, I give the impression I'm pretty loaded. Like I've got a million bucks shoved down my bra everywhere I go, but truth is, Mom and Dad work their butts off for half a paycheck. They don't ever complain about it, and so I try not to be the bitching teenager who begs them for money all the time. They don't know about the clubs, but the cleavage is my ticket in anyway. As for the alcohol—whenever I do drink—someone usually pays for me. Again, thank you cleavage! Who knew, right?

But the salon? Yup, I gotta save up for this stuff. Image people, image.

Clicking my tongue as I wait, I try not to think about Sierra who has been locked in her room until she dies. She hasn't talked to me since the hospital. I've tried to make amends, but really? Shouldn't she be the one groveling for *my* forgiveness? The more I think about it the more upset I get. I'm tempted to turn my head to the side and slap my ear to get rid of the train of thought.

Hope swivels around in her chair, texting her latest boy toy. She giggles every time the phone vibrates.

"Is he taking you to the club tonight?"

She nods and continues to clack away on her keyboard.

"Hey!" I kick her hard in the shin.

"Geez, what?" She laughs and rubs her leg as she tucks her phone away.

"Girl's day, remember?" Hope is usually good at the girl stuff, which is why I *always* pick her over Keira. But today she totally sucks at it.

"Okay, okay. Sorry." She rolls her eyes and throws me a huge grin. "You know how it is though. New flame and all."

Gosh, I thought she'd be used to the new flame crap since she has a new boyfriend about as often as she changes nail polish. Hope's one of those girls who is gorgeous *and* nice… most of the time. I mean, she's nice to your face, but the second you piss her off, she's firing off nasty crap all around school. Like the rest of us I guess.

She's also… fun. Like, I can *almost* be myself with her.

"Alrighty, here we go." Missy stands behind me with the bowl of the perfumed dye. I close my eyes and let her go to work. The process has become so natural I don't even feel the burn in my nose anymore. After a good twenty minutes of slathering the stuff on my head, Missy leads me to the dryer and hands me a few magazines.

"I'll come check on you in a few minutes."

I won't open the magazines. Unless one of them is an Entertainment Weekly on the next Avengers movie, I may take a peek. That's okay to look at in public because that movie is all the rage right now, but if anyone found out I dissect it to death, researching the characteristics of the actors picked to portray each superhero to make sure they got the casting right… yeah, that'll be curtains down on Popular Zoe. And of course, the only magazines they have are ones I only pretend to be interested in.

Hope's now getting slathered herself. Probably going blonder. Damn girl is perfect. Nice rack, pretty face, skinny waist, and long blonde hair. Like Galadriel from Lord of the Rings.

I yank out my cell in the side pocket of my snug jeans, and slide it open to a text.

From Cody.

I miss u.

Gag me. He really needs to take the implied breakup hint. I don't want to ever see that jackass ever again. I blow up my cheeks and let the air come out slowly as my fingers fly across my keyboard.

Stay the hell away from me.

There, if he doesn't get the hint from that, he's an idiot.

My phone buzzes.

Bitch.

Nope, not an idiot. Just a horny prick. Things have never been that way with any guy ever. And I don't want him to look at me, or touch me, or anything. If he tries it again he's losing a testicle.

Hands are suddenly on my shoulders, and I jump back in the seat.

Missy giggles. "Sorry hon, I didn't mean to scare you."

I clutch my chest and try to laugh it off.

"Looks like you'll need a few more minutes," she says prodding my scalp. She plops the dryer back over my head and smiles. "I'll make sure to wave in front of your face or something when I come back."

"Ha ha."

Ten minutes later, it's like my face is on fire. Missy shuts off the dryer and the cold air hits me in a soothing wave of relief.

"Ooo!" she squeals. "It's gonna look real pretty, Zoe."

I nod and she leads me to the sink. I close my eyes and involuntarily moan as she washes my hair. Oh my gosh, this is the best part. Her fingers massage my scalp and the warmth of the water sends me into an intoxicating state of bliss. Ah yeah. No Sierra, no Cody, no persona. Just me in a luxurious bath.

Then a face snaps behind my eyes. I'm not alone in my paradise here, and I'm not sure if I'm happy or upset to see his dark eyes, his dark brown hair falling slightly in front of them, his boyish grin as he strokes my lips with his thumb, the muscles in his arms flexing as he moves his hand to wrap around the back of my neck, his long eyelashes brushing underneath his eyes as he closes them, his lips parting and coming closer…

The squeak of the water faucet jolts me back to the salon. My face is warm, actually my entire body is flushed, and I have to calm my breathing.

What is wrong with me?

"Did you enjoy that?" I look at Missy who is stifling a huge grin, and I gaze around the salon as I hear several sniggers. Hope is keeled over in a fit, wiping her eyes.

I don't know if it's possible to send all the blood in your body up to your face, but I'm sure that's what happens to me.

"Um… yeah." Oh man. How loud was I moaning?

"Come on." Missy giggles and pulls me to the styling chair.

I plunge into an agonizing hour of being locked in the seat while several people whisper around me and steal amused glances in my direction. Hope keeps winking at me, and I'm ready to sock her perfect nose in.

That's not even the worst part. Zak will not leave my thoughts, no matter how hard I try to shut the door on him. He's just so… swoon! I wish I could give him a popular makeover like all those movies so we could be friends in public. But knowing Zak, that totally wouldn't fly. Besides, he wouldn't be *Zak* anymore. And that would suck. Having two personalities is tough business. Worth it, but it's not for everybody.

I'm done before Hope, but I don't have to wait long. We primp ourselves in the mirror, throwing out compliments to each other, though it seems pretty fake.

"Really, Zoe. You're totally sexy as a redhead. Cody will be falling all over himself when he sees it."

This is how distant my friends are from me. I haven't said a word to him since last week, and no one has noticed.

"Yeah."

She gives me a look. Oh right. I'm supposed to be agreeing or something.

"Looks like it'll be a club night for me too." I force a smile. "No way am I letting this hair go to waste."

"That's what happens when you don't use the cheap stuff." Missy grins as she rings me up.

I roll my eyes and pay her, wishing I could give her a bigger tip, but I can't really afford it.

Hope links elbows with me and speed walks through the parking lot.

"What's the rush?" I say as I try not to fall face first on the asphalt. Heels aren't good for walking, but they are rule number three.

"You'll see." She's grinning from ear to ear, and I can't help but reciprocate. I love it when Hope is like this. Like we're really friends and she wouldn't care if I suddenly spouted off Doctor Who trivia.

But she would, so I keep my mouth shut.

We hop in her car. (Cute sports car that looks like the one Sierra wrecked, only Hope's brand-new where as I got mine from my grandma. Sigh. I miss my car.) Then she takes off toward my house. She's the craziest driver in the world I swear, so I close my eyes and pretend I'm traveling by Transport Tube.

"Okay, close your eyes!" Hope says, not noticing my lids are already clamped tight.

The car jerks to a stop and I hear Hope unbuckle. "Okay, you stay here and I'll be right back."

I give a fake impatient sigh but smile. I'm a sucker for surprises.

After a few minutes, my door opens and a hand wraps around my wrist, pulling me out.

"You can open your eyes now!"

Mom is out here in the driveway and shouts, "Ta Da!"

I'm really trying to be happy about it. The car is shiny and it's silver, which isn't a bad color, but it's old. Like, 'Watch out! Old lady on the road!' old. Compared to my cute sports car Sierra wrecked, this is a downgrade. And not good for my social status.

But Hope looks happy about it. So maybe it's not as bad as I think.

I give Mom a forced smile. "For me?"

She nods so fast I think her head might jiggle off her neck. She hands me the key and I can't hide my shaking hand.

Why am I such a brat? She bought me a car! I try to snap myself out of the bad attitude. It's not her fault I humiliated myself with sex noises in front of twenty strangers. And definitely not her fault she gave birth to the devil. AKA, my sister.

I cozy into the driver's seat as she bounces in next to me. Hope crawls in the backseat and squeals. The interior is nice, it's clean, and who can't love a new car? Now I'm squealing too. My smile isn't forced anymore as I shove the key in the ignition.

Nothing.

I look down, trying to figure out what the crap I'm doing wrong. When I rest my hand on the shifter, my stomach drops.

"Um, Mom?"

"Yes?"

"You bought me a manual?"

She nods.

"Did it cross your mind I may not know how to drive this thing?"

"There's no better way to learn." She's still smiling, and I'm trying real hard not to break down. I'm so not talented enough for this, and I can't even imagine driving this thing to school without making a fool of myself. I blow up my cheeks and close my eyes.

Mom lets out a huge sigh. "Zoe, I'm sorry. I wish we could have gotten you a car you wanted, but this was the only one we could afford that wasn't on its last leg."

I stay quiet, imitating a blowfish.

"We'll teach you how to drive it. It's not hard."

All the air I've been holding in my cheeks explodes out. "When? You and Dad are so busy. Hardly ever home."

She seems to be struggling with the answer. I raise my eyebrows exaggerating my point.

"We'll try to make ourselves more available, but I'm sure some of your friends know how to drive a stick." She gazes back at Hope who shrugs.

I guffaw which is so unattractive, but I don't care right now.

She ignores my dismissive laugh. "What about Keira?"

"No."

"Does Cody know how?" Hope asks.

Ugh. "No."

Mom sits biting her lip for a minute. Then a huge gasp of revelation fills the car.

"Zak! You can ask him. He drives that truck."

I think I'm going to die. In fact I can feel the combustion starting in my gut. *Fake it Zoe, fake it! Hope is in the backseat and she can't know you even talk to him.* "Ew. No."

"Why not?"

"We're not friends, Mom."

"Doesn't he take you to school?"

Oh gosh. "Just that one time. I walk."

"Well, it was just a suggestion," she spits. Great, now she's upset. "Be happy when you're father gets home. He's really excited about this, and he's trying to say he's sorry for yelling at you."

She gets out of the car, leaving me feeling like the horrible person I am. I wish I could escape my company too.

"Um," Hope stutters, "I'm gonna head out."

I nod and try to push back my tears. Maybe pretending to be a bitch has made me into a real one.

"I'll see you later."

And she's gone.

I crawl in the backseat and curl up, letting my styled hair fall over my face. The smell of the dye mixed with the fruity shampoo fills my nostrils, and I almost get high off it.

You know what sucks? I want to talk to Zak. I want to start spewing some nerdy crap and laugh and stuff. Hope is good to chill with but she's not who I need to feel better right now.

Maybe I can ask him. I mean, it would make my parents happy. And Hope saw how I initially reacted so I could come up with some excuse if she found out.

I sit up and look at his house, stomach knotting with the idea of going over there. Do I really want to risk it? I could ask around school to see if anyone higher on the social ladder is available to teach me.

But do I really want that?

No.

I want him.

Sexy nerdboy.

My breath fogs up the car window as I huff. Why are stupid decisions like this hard?

I huff again.

Because I make them that way.

Chapter 5

Being smooth is not my thing.

If I blow any more air into my cheeks, they may pop. I can't believe I'm actually going to do this. If anyone catches me driving Zak around, the rumors will zoom through the air about me hooking up with King of the Dorks. But I've got it all planned out.

Excuse number one, my parents are making me.

Excuse number two, I'm grounded from all my friends, so this was the only way I can learn.

Excuse number three, I'm sleep walking.

Now that I've got my social butt covered, I just gotta ask him. And this is what's making my cheeks sore.

I've never asked Zak for anything before. Even when we were besties. He always offered so I never had to. And after I totally ditched him and treated him like he has a good case of dragonpox, I'm scared out of my mind.

What if he says no?

I let all the air out, my bangs fluttering across my forehead. *Zoe, just get this over with!*

Another pumpkin imitation later, and I'm knocking on his

door. I want to beeline for the bushes, but my legs feel like gummy worms.

The lock clicks and there he stands in his holey jeans and holding an Xbox controller, with a look that says I stunned the crap out of him.

"Uh, hey." Smooth, Zoe, real smooth.

He doesn't say anything. His mouth is doing that opening and closing thing like the clowns on a miniature golf course. He looks over my head and out to the street.

What do I do? Just walk away? Wave my hand in front of his face? Crap myself?

"What... what are you doing here?" His ears go red and the controller slips from his hand.

I hear a car go by behind me and BAM! All my insecurities rush into my thoughts. Even though Zak looks freaking amazing in his Yoshi shirt, I can't be seen at *his* house.

Oh gosh.

"Can I come in?" The words are out so fast, and I don't even wait for an answer. I squeeze past him and shut the door behind me.

He chuckles. "Yeah, I guess you can."

I laugh... a huge dorky and nervous laugh as I look around his house. Not much has changed since last time I was here. Well, physically. It wasn't this awkward between me and him, but that's totally my fault.

"So, uh..." he stutters as he picks up the controller he dropped. "You need something?"

"Yes, I..." I kink my neck to look behind him. "You stuck?"

"Huh?"

I point to the TV screen. "Minas Tirith. That's a tough level, and it looks like you're out of ammo."

He smirks, and scratches the back of his neck with the controller before tossing it on the couch. "It's been a while since I played it, and I can't remember the code for infinite missiles. I was gonna go Google the code for it—"

"X, X, down, B." Holy Hulk! I totally said that out loud.

Zak's mouth pops open and his ears go red again. "I-I think you're right."

He picks the controller back up and enters in the code. The small *shink* sound lets him know he now has unlimited firepower.

"Nice!" He throws me that really sexy smile and I don't believe it, but I'm moving to sit next to him.

"Y, up, Y, down makes it so one hit will kill them. May help you when you're trying to get those ladders taken care of." I wink and he nudges me with his elbow.

And now I've lost my train of thought.

"Thanks," he says, entering in the code. He sets the controller down and shifts so he's angled toward me. I can't take my eyes off his, even though they aren't exactly looking at me. They're so dark though. Like almost black so it's like one giant pupil. And his dark brown hair is all flopped across his forehead. I want to reach up and feel how soft it is.

"Uh, Zo?"

Sigh...

"Yeah?"

"Did you need something?"

Oh right! I did come over here for a reason other than drooling over him.

"Yes, sorry. I was wondering… I mean I don't know if you noticed, but my parents bought me a new car."

"Cool."

"It's a manual, and I was hoping…" Hoping? Who the heck is talking here? I sound like a bumbling idiot. "Will you teach me how to drive it?"

His face loses all its color, and he wipes his palms on his jeans. After a few seconds he finally makes eye contact with me, giving me another sexy grin. "Tell you what. You beat this level for me, and I'll teach you how to drive."

The blinds are shut, and it looks like Zak's mom is on duty tonight. It's just me and him. And since I've already spouted off codes, playing the game won't make me any more of a nerd. Besides, the geeky stuff seems to be getting me a lot more attention from him than my underwear dancing.

"I haven't played in a long time."

Yeah, that's a total lie.

He chuckles and slaps the controller in my hand, his fingers lingering on my skin. The hairs on my arm shoot straight up.

"You just told me a code I didn't know, and I played two months ago."

I tap my forehead. "Good memory."

He cocks his eyebrow, making me fumble with the controller.

"Well, beat it, or there's no deal."

Slouching back on the couch, interlocking his fingers and resting his head on his hands, he gives me a good impression of someone who's trying to look cool, but not sure if they're doing it right.

He's *so* doing it right.

"I get to be Gandalf."

Video games are total time suckers, but they are so worth it! I have no idea how long it's been, but it's dark outside when I finally toss the controller back at Zak, who is now sitting so close his hips are touching mine.

"And that is how it's done." I smile.

He tosses his head back, barking out his laughter and clapping. It's so darn cute I want to jump into his arms and smack one right there on the kisser.

Instead I throw out a random question so I don't lose what's left of my mind. "What time is it?"

"Almost ten. Ariana should be here any…"

Thump! Thump!

"…minute." He gives me a smile before he stands.

Ariana? What the hell? Why is she…?

Dammit! The documentary! I totally spaced it.

"Wait!" I rush to Zak before he gets to the door. No one at school can know I was here for… oh my gosh, it's been four hours. "Um… do you mind if I…" Great, how do I get out of this one?

"Can I use your bathroom?"

He chuckles. "You know where it is, silly girl."

Ignoring the flippity flop my stomach does, I book it to the bathroom and lock the door before Zak can get the front door open.

Trying to be quiet in panic mode is near impossible. I get the shower curtain open and move all the shampoo and soap bottles out of the window sill so I can make a break for it. Gym has paid off in the pull up department for me. I wiggle myself through the window and fall flat on my ass in Ms. Gibbons tulips.

Zak is totally going to figure it out since I'm not covering my tracks, but it's not like I can put things back the way they were. And I'm too busy freaking out to care right now.

I stand to wipe off the crusted mud all over the butt of my jeans when I hear Zak's voice carry through the living room window.

"I invited her."

"Why the hell would you do that?"

Yikes! I haven't heard someone use that type of tone when they were talking about me since… well, since Geek Zoe roamed the halls.

Ariana's a girl in our grade, way below the status of chess club player. She usually has lipstick on her teeth, and her blonde hair is rarely done in anything but a ragged ponytail. She's got the most annoying laugh; it's more of a *hardy har har*. Like she's heckling you every time you say something funny. She's got about a million zits on her nose alone, and right now, *she's* ready to talk shit about *me*.

I feel sick.

"Because she's into that stuff. She just played four hours of Lord of the Rings with me."

"Did she need something from you?"

It's quiet long enough for me to panic over what Zak's face looks like. I'm almost willing to peek around the corner so I can see, but then I remember his blinds are shut.

Zak mumbles something I don't catch, and Ariana starts laughing.

"Okay, okay. I'll be nice. But if she does anything bitchy, I swear, I'm socking her in her overstuffed boob."

I wait for more conversation... more gossip really, but they start comparing notes on how difficult the different levels are on the game I just beat. I'm pretty sure Zak has taken out his notebook filled with all the theories we put in there about if Gimli had the speed of Legolas than his stats would be higher.

If Ariana wasn't in there—totally wrong in her theories, by the way—I'd be sitting next to Zak talking nerd. I guess she's saving me from going full out Geek Zoe.

Still, I'm a wee bit jealous.

Okay, a lot jealous.

Before I can cause any more social damage, I sprint back home.

Chapter 6

Why can't my bad decisions only affect me?

The cafeteria is like the Houses in Harry Potter, I swear. Where you sit is uber important. Because I'm part of the popular group, we don't have a designated spot. We pick and choose depending on the day and if we've decided to eat off campus or not. Everyone revolves around us.

Except for one table.

The Dungeons and Dragons table.

Zak's table.

If this was middle school, it would be my table too.

Lunch is split in two. I'm in the later lunch with a few of my friends, but Hope is in the earlier lunch. So I park my butt next to Keira for some girl talk before all the guys get here.

"Where were *you* on Friday?" Keira gives me that you-totally-hooked-up-and-ditched-your-friends-look. I take a deep breath and put on my fake smile. It's like I have to triple act around her so she likes me. She's a jealous one. Not saying I'm hotter or anything, but the boys tend to flock toward me and Hope more than her, and she seems a little bitter about it.

"Got my butt grounded." Excuse number two is what I decide to go with.

"How'd you pull that one off?" Keira takes a sip of her diet soda and strokes the top of her cleavage with her fingertips. I think it's out of habit now. A guy from third period walks by not even pretending he doesn't notice her doing this.

"Being a bitch to my nosey parents." I roll my eyes to keep up with the act. My parents are anything but nosey, but according to Popular Zoe, parents are evil people who want to take control of every aspect of their child's life.

"That sucks." Though she sounds like she doesn't care. Her eyes flick toward Cody across the cafeteria and mine follow. He's got his arm around his next victim and when he catches me staring, he rams his tongue in her mouth.

"Sexy." Keira laughs. "I take it you two aren't... you two anymore?"

I'm so not talking about the freaky attack with her. I mean, if I wouldn't even tell Hope...

"Well, it's been a month."

"Oh wow. I didn't realize you two had been together that long. You're right. Time for fresh meat."

She gazes around the cafeteria, and I'm happy she's momentarily distracted so I don't have to talk about my ex.

Douchebag.

"Is there a guy here you haven't dated?"

I force a giggle. "There are lots, but I'd rather gouge my eyes out than kiss any of them."

She nods. "I know, right? But there must be someone…"

She's still scoping out the room, her eyes hungry for the next Mr. Livingston.

"Well, there's Levi," she says after a minute, pointing at him from across the cafeteria. He's got his drumsticks out—like always—and patting a beat against his legs. His smile is pretty cute. But he's two years younger, so I'm surprised Keira mentions him at all.

"He's a sophomore."

"Yeah, but look at him. He's got the muscles, the eyes, and the hair. He plays the drums. And I mean look at his feet. If anything you've got something *very* satisfying to look forward to."

I burst out laughing, which isn't very attractive, but I can't help it. "Why don't you take a stab at him, then?"

"I already have three boyfriends. A fourth will complicate things."

And three *isn't* complicated. Yeah. Sounds like Keira. I shake my head. "I don't think Levi is my type." Yeah, my type watches Spiderman documentaries and wears a Star Wars keychain.

"Fine. We'll find a shrimp for you." She straightens in her seat to scan the room again.

"There's a lot more pickens for you in this department." She laughs. "I mean, have a go at anyone at the Dungeons and Doofus' table."

I get to my knees to get a better look at the scrawny nerds, all leaning over their game board. I don't let anyone know of course, but I could totally whoop their butts at D&D, and I kind of want to.

I give a fake shudder as I settle back down in the booth. "I think I threw up a bit." Total bull.

Keira giggles and takes another sip of her drink. "Well, let me know which one you want to deflower. I'll make a public announcement."

I chuck my crumpled napkin at her.

"Shut up." I grimace at her before getting up and walking to the main cafeteria doors. The guys we hang with are grouped there, and I'd much rather talk to them than her right now.

I only make it about three steps before I hear my name being shouted across the room.

"Yo! Zoe!" Levi jogs up, jamming his drumsticks in the side pocket of his khakis. "Hey I heard you and Cody broke up."

Subtle.

"What gave you that idea?" I ask, the sarcasm soaking my tone as I gesture to the tongue-dancing across the room.

He smiles. Wowza. He's pretty smoking hot actually. My stomach does a little flip, but it's a somersault compared to the backhand spring I get from when Zak smiles. Darn boy.

"You okay? You want to talk about it?"

I glance behind him at Keira, who winks at me. Word around here spreads faster than the Enterprise at Warp-10. I'm sure our conversation was heard by twenty people around us, catching up to Levi within seconds. Hence, why he stands in front of me, waiting to be rebound boy.

I flick my gaze to Cody, who's glaring at me. I get a sick satisfaction from his anger. It's like I can punish him by throwing myself at someone else.

"I don't really want to talk," I say, taking a step closer to Levi, making my intentions clear. He raises his eyebrows, and his mouth pops open in audible shock.

"Uh… wh-what do you want to do then?"

Get back at the dickwad who attacked me.

I roll my eyes and get on my tippy toes to reach him. I smack a gooey kiss on his lips and pull him close.

The only thing going on in my head right now is the look I imagine on Cody's face. I bet he's seething at my public display with some kid I've talked to maybe twice in my whole life.

I know I'm a total bitch for using Levi like this. But that's who I am in school. A bitch. A bitch who gets asked out and ogled and fawned over. A complete act that's getting easier and easier the longer I'm in it.

I don't even notice Levi's frenching me until someone taps on my arm and I have to extract my tongue from his mouth.

"I'm a pretty tolerant teacher, but this isn't exactly appropriate during school hours."

Ms. Weber's interruption sort of brings me back to life. Why am I so stupid? This isn't going to fix anything.

I glance around the room. Cody's mouth is turned down in disgust, but he's looking at Levi like he feels sorry for him, not angry. But that isn't what throws me over the edge.

It's Zak.

He's standing by the D&D table, looking at me with such loathing I can't seem to concentrate on anything else. He crosses his arms over his chest, his muscles intensely frozen. His friends try to get his attention back to the game, but he ignores them, storming across the cafeteria and out onto the school grounds. He heads for the bleachers, with Ariana following shortly after.

"Miss Livingston." Ms. Weber is still waiting for me to untangle myself from Levi.

I take a step away from him and mumble an apology, and before I permanently turn red from embarrassment, I bolt out the doors after Zak.

Chapter 7

If there is any more touchy feely crap, I'm going

to kill her.

I can't talk to him. Not here. Not where everyone can see me. I'm pretty sure no one noticed me staring, or following him, but I can't risk it.

So I'll eavesdrop instead. He's sitting in the middle section of the bleachers with Ariana, and my stomach plummets into my feet making it hard to walk. Why is he with *her*... again? I sneak around back and crouch underneath the seats and try to keep my footfalls quiet, though it's really hard wearing heels. And no way am I taking them off with all the trash on the ground. Sick.

"Are you seriously giving me the silent treatment?" Ariana sighs and stares Zak down. She's wearing a skirt so I can see straight up it, giving me full access to purple granny panties. I cringe and try to keep my eyes on Zak. I guess it's better than a thong though. I do not want to see a full moon.

"What?"

"You're not talking because you're upset about her, right?"

Zak shrugs.

"And you're taking it out on me?" She inches closer to him, and I feel like yanking her hair out.

"Sorry." He moves his backpack so it's nestled between them. He's pretty smooth about it, but I can tell he doesn't want to be close to her.

"You know I hate it when you shut me out."

I hear a grinding noise and it takes a minute for me to register it's my teeth. How long has she been his "go to" girl?

"Sorry," he says again. "I know." Zak picks at a loose thread in his jeans, and it's quiet for what seems like an eternity. "I thought, after this weekend, things were getting better."

This weekend? Does he mean after I pulled a fugitive move out his bathroom window?

"Zak…" She scoots closer still, almost sitting on top of Zak's bag. I really want to scream at her to take the hint.

"Don't."

"What?" Ariana's hands are on his forearm now.

"Don't say it."

"Say what?"

"You know what."

She lets out a huge breath from her nostrils. "I don't get why you let her do this to you."

"She just gets to me!" Zak's arms fly up and Ariana pulls away. "I don't know why either, but she does. And I don't know how much more of it I can take."

"Then don't take it anymore!" I see Zak's surprise as Ariana yells back. I have to admit, I've never heard her voice this loud either.

"But…" He can't seem to finish his thought.

"Come on. She's not worth this and you know it. You *have* to drop it." Her voice softens. "She's not your friend anymore. You have to let her go." She rubs his back to soothe him.

"Don't you think I've tried? It's harder than it looks." He shrugs her hand off, and I can't help but feel happy he keeps rejecting her touch. If he hadn't, I probably would've gone all Gollum on her even though I have no claim on the boy.

Ariana's face darkens, flushing to the color of a fire engine. "I guess if you're into shallow girls who sleep with every guy they see, I suppose she would be hard to get over. But I thought you were different than that. Better."

Holy Batman. Maybe I'm not exactly popular with everyone. I've changed almost one-hundred percent and people are still talking about me behind my back.

My cheeks blow up, and I force the tears away.

Breathe, Zoe. Breathe! You have to breathe!

I can't, though. It hurts too much. It's like it's two years ago again, and I'm right back to where I was. Being insulted and gossiped about. It doesn't matter Ariana's one of the loser girls. It feels close to the same as it did before. Only this time, she's making fun of someone I'm *trying* to be, and not who I really am.

I guess that's not as bad.

I'm breathing again.

I'm also trying not to notice Ariana said "get over." I had no idea he had to get over anyone, let alone someone who hasn't given him the time of day since middle school. Someone like... *me.*

"Don't believe everything you hear. I know she's not really like that."

There goes my heart again, pumping so loud I wish I could turn it on mute.

"You keep saying that, but I think you're in denial."

"She's not like that." His voice isn't mean, but it gives the impression he's done talking about it.

How the heck does he know I'm not really like that? Just from this weekend? Or do I always revert to Geek Zoe around him?

"Well, you need to face facts," Ariana says, standing. She stumbles a little and Zak reaches out to steady her. When she gets her bearings, she folds her arms. "She's changed. She's a slut who doesn't think about anyone but herself. She doesn't want anything to do with you because you like things that aren't 'socially acceptable'." With every syllable of her air quoted words, she cocks her head to the side. I'm about ready to reach up and yank her skirt down, just to watch her face get red. See how she feels when someone humiliates her. But that would make me a major hypocrite. "It's stupid and shallow and weak. And you deserve better than that." She pauses to catch her breath. Zak looks at the football field, seemingly lost in thought. "I hate to be the one who has to keep knocking sense into you, but someone has to."

He nods.

Crap. He's not defending me this time. Why would he? Ariana's... *right.*

She's right.

Oh my gosh.

I *am* a huge-ass hypocrite.

Stabbing pains shoot all over my body. I'm about to buckle over, but the ground is so nasty.

Ariana clomps down the bleachers, leaving Zak alone. Should I say something to him? How do I do that without him knowing I was here this whole time?

The warning bell rings, and I know I have to go. I can't be late for my last class, but my feet aren't moving. Zak punches his bag before picking it up, and tromps off after Ariana.

Hope gives me a ride home. I'm so glad I found her before I found Keira. I don't want to act anymore, and though I still have to hide everything in the Harry Potter closet in my mind, I can at least somewhat be myself with Hope.

I stuff my Chemistry book between my legs as I buckle in. I haven't spoken a word to anyone since lunch, and Hope eyes me with a tentative smirk.

"I heard about Levi." Hope is anything but subtle.

I nod.

"Does he taste as good as he looks?"

I nod again. I'm not interested in gossip, and I'm *way* beyond putting up my false persona. I want to get home and erase the conversation I overheard.

"Could you feel it?"

Oh my gosh, is she serious? I give her a look and she's stifling a huge grin. "Are the rumors about him true?" She's laughing now, and I finally break down in a fit too.

"I really have no idea how big his wang is since I wasn't paying attention."

"Ah! I knew it!" she says slamming her hand on the steering wheel.

"Knew what?" I still can't stop laughing.

"I could get you to crack a smile." She winks. "Now tell me what's wrong."

I'm a freaking horrible person who made out with some random guy before stumbling after a guy who I'm face over feet for and I don't know why. And I just... I miss being *me*.

I end up shrugging and looking out the window. Would Hope understand? Or would she be the next person to spit out a bunch of stuff behind my back?

"Are you surfin' the Red Sea or something? You're really quiet, girl."

"Sorry." And then using her question as an excuse I say, "And yes, I'm on my period. So I'm just a little out of it today."

"I guess I'd be upset too if I was PMS-ing on top of breaking up with my boyfriend, my sister crashing my uber cute sports car, and then getting grounded for... how long was it?"

Oh that's right. I'm "grounded."

"Who knows? My dad didn't get to that part."

"I'm sorry. Is there anything I can do?"

No.

Well, maybe.

"Give me a hug?"

She smiles as she pulls over bumping against the curb. "Whoops," she says her face flushing. Even if she did drive stick, I don't think I'd ask her to teach me.

We hop out and she pulls me in her arms. I guess faking to be someone else *has* worked. I know I wouldn't have her if I still hung out with Zak and all the other D&D players.

We pull back and I smile.

"Thanks for the ride, dirty skank."

She laughs and socks my arm. "No problem, slut. See ya tomorrow."

She drives off, leaving me standing in my front yard, heels sinking into the grass. I flick my eyes to my new car and puff up my face.

If I was a nice person, I'd leave Zak alone. Ignore what I overheard today and move on. Do what I've been doing. Be friends with Hope, keep getting the attention I want, and minimize getting tormented by all the kids in school.

But I'm not a nice person. I'm an egotistical, stuck-up, selfish beast. That's who I've become. And all I can think about is what Ariana said. "*You have to drop it. You have to let her go.*"

I don't *want* Zak to let me go. Not when I just found out he had to. The problem is, I don't know why I feel like this. It's not like I can be his friend without suffering the consequences.

I let out the air stuck in my face and walk down the sidewalk.

I'm going to talk to Zak. And this time, I won't crawl out his window to get away from him.

Chapter 8

Only Zak would reference Star Wars during a

driving lesson.

Thunk, thunk, thunk.

Oh gosh. I think my stomach has fallen into my butt permanently as I stand at his door. I'm trying not to blow up my face, knowing how stupid I'd look if he caught me.

He opens the door smiling, but when he sees me, his face falls. He doesn't say anything.

"Uh, hey." How lame am I?

He narrows his eyes. "What do you want, Zoe?"

He's still mad. He should be. From how I left on Friday or what I did at lunch I'm not sure. And I stammer out my next sentence. "I-I wanted to say I'm... like, I'm totally sorry about leaving the way I did on Friday."

His eyebrow goes up and his ears go red. "Yeah?"

"Yeah. That wasn't cool of me. And I don't really have a good excuse for it."

He shrugs and moves to lean against the door frame, but misses and falls smack into me.

I'm trying real hard not to laugh, but I'm not successful. When he stabilizes himself he moves about ten feet away from me, but I can still feel the heat coming from his face.

"Uh…" He stumbles over the small syllable. "D-did you need something else?"

My breath catches as he jams his hands in his pockets. His holey jeans look so damn good on him. Usually, I'm always focused on his feathery hair and those dark eyes. And his jaw line is so chiseled, I can see the muscles contract as he chomps his teeth together, waiting for one of us to continue the conversation. Even his Fallout shirt under his black plaid does it for me.

"Zo?"

I shift my eyes, hoping he didn't notice me checking him out. "I wondered if you were still okay teaching me how to drive?"

"I thought you were grounded."

That lie is really starting to bite me in the butt. "I-I just can't see any of my friends." Crap. That totally came out wrong. "I mean—"

"No, you're right," he says not looking at me. "We're not friends."

Ouchy. I wish I could argue, but I can't. I haven't been his friend. Gave that up when I gave up everything. I gulp and ask again, "So, can you? You know, teach me?"

He hesitates which makes me almost mumble out a whole bunch of "you don't have to if you don't want to, but I'd really like you to's" but I bite my tongue. I can't control the natural response I have to awkward silence, and my face blows up to the size of a giant water balloon.

He smirks at my cheeks and pinches them together. My stomach does that stupid backhand spring like he's suddenly the center of my universe.

"Hey Mom!" His sudden outburst makes me jump and he laughs at me. "It okay if I take Zoe out for a drive?"

He makes it sound like a date. I'm not the only one who thinks so either. Mrs. Gibbons sticks her head out into the entryway, a gleaming smile glued on her face.

"Oh hi Zoe! I didn't know you were here. Zak, honey, aren't you going to invite her in?"

"We were going to head out," he says, giving her a look I can't see.

"Will you be home for dinner?"

"Yeah."

"Is Zoe joining us?"

"No."

I only see half the conversation, but Zak obviously gives her the please-don't-embarrass-me look.

"Okay. You kids have fun!" Her excitement is so transparent, it makes me feel like I should explain, but Zak pulls me down the porch steps before I can squeeze it in.

"Sorry," he mutters as he drops his hand from my arm. I kind of wish he would've kept it there. Like old times. Like with his other... oh that's right. We're not friends.

"You don't have to apologize. I know she *adores* me." I nudge him with my elbow—because I just have to touch him—and he smirks.

"Must be because you're so humble about it."

"Hey, you know you want this." I gesture to my body in a teasing and completely unsexy way. Zak throws his head back in a fit of laughter, which causes me to giggle like a little school girl. We better get in the car fast before someone sees Geek Zoe.

"Yes. So humble." He walks over to my car, right to the driver's side. I make my way to the passenger seat.

"Um, hello? Where are you going?" There's that smile again, sending waves of tiny butterflies in my chest.

"You walked to the driver's seat. I thought you were going to take me somewhere secluded so I don't kill anyone."

His barking laugh is so addictive. "I was opening your door for you, silly girl."

"Oh." I'm so stupid. I cross around, and he holds the door open. "I guess chivalry isn't dead."

"For some of us it isn't."

He shuts the door and walks over to his side. Gosh, I'm freaking nervous. My hands shake so badly you could put a paint can in them and I'd have it mixed within seconds. And he called me "silly girl" again. Why the heck does that make my heart go *wa-bam*?

He sits and a wave of his amazing cologne hits my nostrils. I resist the urge to moan.

"Okay," he says as he buckles. "You ready?"

Heart still going way too fast. Maybe this isn't such a good idea. But I nod anyway.

"You've got your foot on the clutch?"

I nod. I know *that* much about manuals.

"Let's start her up."

I can't get the stupid key in. My hands won't stop shaking. Zak smiles, reaches over, brushing my hand and turns the key.

The car vibrates up my butt and I let out a yelp.

Zak grins, totally holding back his laughter and says, "Nice. What kind of engine does this have?"

I shrug. I don't think my voice can function right now.

"Okay, let's put the car in reverse." He looks down at the shifter and laughs. "You've got a funky one."

"What?"

"You see the 'R'?"

I look down, squinting at the tiny letter in the upper left corner next to the number '1'. "Yeah."

"Well, that means you have to push the shifter down before going in gear. Watch me, and keep your foot on the clutch."

He shifts so fast I blink a couple times before saying, "Wait. Show me again."

He chuckles as he pulls it out of gear, then back in. "Did you see that time?"

I throw him a look. "Yes."

"Okay, now feather the clutch."

"I wanna what now?"

He shakes his head, stifling his laughter… again. "Do you remember on *Star Wars*…?"

"You're seriously going to go there?" Now I'm stifling some

major giggles.

"Let me finish. Millennium Falcon. Does Han Solo whip the lever down when he puts it in hyper drive?"

I totally know the answer. I still watch it every other week. But am I ready to be one hundred percent Geek Zoe? Well, maybe right now. I mean, we're not in school. And I know Zak won't make fun of me or anything.

"No. He does it kinda slow."

"That's feathering. Ease your foot off the clutch."

Okay, so the Star Wars reference works. Darn boy knows me better than I know myself. I "feather" the clutch, my foot shaking either from nerves or the vibrating engine, and the car rolls back.

I pull my foot off the clutch, startled from the sudden movement and the car lurches to a stop.

"It moved!"

Zak bends over cackling between his legs. "It's supposed to move, Zo." He wipes tears from his eyes. My defenses pop in, but I can't help but laugh with him, so I know he's not going to take me seriously.

"Well, I'm sorry. I got scared. There are too many things to concentrate on. Shifting and the clutch, not to mention all the other stuff like the speed limit and you know, people in the road." I shake my head, trying to get the smile off my face. "I can't do this."

"Relax, Zo. This is your first attempt. Everyone stalls. I still do sometimes."

"There's too much crap going on," I say folding my arms across my waist, my smile finally disappearing. I don't feel like embarrassing myself anymore today. Especially in front of him.

"Tell you what. Put your hand on the shifter."

I glare at him.

"Just do it. Trust me."

I huff, but I slam my hand down on the stupid thing.

"Okay," he says before setting his hand on mine. He weaves his fingers in between my own, and I swear I swallowed a drummer with the way my heart pounds in my throat. I steal a glance at him, and he looks like he's about to sweat a rainstorm. "I-I'll shift, you worry about the clutch." He gulps and his grip tightens on my hand.

If he thinks this is less distracting, he's dead wrong.

He goes to start the car for me again, leaning so close his breath tickles my neck. My head goes fuzzy as I picture him closing the distance between our bodies, forgetting I'm supposed to be doing something. His lips form words, but I don't hear them. His scent is intoxicating, pulling me under. Holy crap! I'm going to pass out!

"Zo?"

"Huh?"

He chuckles. "Did you hear me?"

"Um, sorry what?"

"I need your foot on the clutch to start the car."

I shake my head, wishing the fuzziness would wear off, but he smiles, and it makes everything blurry.

Somehow I concentrate enough to press my foot down. He starts the engine and leans back, taking the mouthwatering air with him. He moves my hand on the shifter.

"All right, take the Millennium Falcon into hyper drive."

I chuckle and ease out the clutch. When the car moves this time, I don't jump.

"What do I do when I get to the road?" I ask as I near the end of my driveway.

"Push down on the clutch, put your foot on the brake, and wait for me to shift."

Whoa. Lot of words. "What?!"

"Don't freak out. You're doing fine."

The car bumps off the curb as I turn onto the road. I try to remember what he said, but in my haste I put the clutch through the floor and slam on the brake.

At least the car's still running.

Zak doesn't say anything about my jerky stop, but purses his lips together and shakes with silent chuckles. He moves my hand.

"Do it again."

If he means stall, I comply.

"Sorry."

"Don't apologize, it'll happen more than once. Try again." He leans over me to start the car. I consider stalling it on purpose if he's going to come this close to me when I do.

I'm pretty good once the car gets going. Shifting from first to second to third isn't as hard as when I come to a complete stop and start going again. I try to avoid stop signs and traffic lights.

"Pull into this parking lot," Zak says pointing out my window.

I do, then park the car in a spot overlooking a giant field.

I cut the engine the way I'm supposed to this time. Zak releases his hold on my hand, and I realize how sweaty his must've been because the breeze instantly catches on my skin.

"Ready to do it by yourself?" he asks, gazing around the vacant lot. "Pretty sure you won't kill anyone out here."

I want to give him a playful punch in the arm, but I'm still too nervous... slash, exhilarated from the drive.

"Maybe in a minute." Crap. My voice totally shakes.

"Are you okay?"

I nod.

"Really, you did just fine. Especially for your first time."

I lean back on the headrest, taking deep breaths. If only he knew it isn't just the driving making me all flustered and crazy.

The tension in the car must make him flustered too, because he stammers out his next question, which comes out of nowhere.

"So, you and Levi, huh?"

Chapter 9

Hi Zoe. It's Zoe. We haven't spoken for a while.

"It's not like that," I say, opening my eyes and grinning. I can't help but feel happy he's interested, even though I feel more guilty about the whole make-out with random guy thing.

"Not like what?"

"We're not dating or anything."

He puckers his forehead and his dark eyes narrow. Whoops, maybe not the right thing to say.

"You always kiss guys you aren't dating?"

Yeah, definitely not the right thing to say. I can hear the double meaning behind the question and my insides turn to mulch. "It was just… a mistake. That's all. I've had a bad week."

That's the understatement of the year.

"Want to talk about it?"

Yes. I want to be back in his living room with the Nintendo controller, spilling my guts about how fake and stupid I am, how Cody assaulted me, and how every night I cover myself and read comic books. But nothing escapes my tongue. It's too much, and I'm not allowed to dump it on him. Since he's not my friend and all.

"I'm sorry I asked," he says, shifting in his seat. "I just—"

"Worry?" A smile forms on my lips, but I don't look at him.

"Yeah."

"Why?" I keep my eyes locked on a speck on the window.

"Why what?"

"Why do you worry about me?"

I hate it when he hesitates. Every breath I take during the silence I get more and more self-conscious and question why I say the stupid things I say.

"I dunno. I guess I-I'll always worry about you, Zo."

It doesn't answer my question, but I don't care. I can't help the smile that glues onto my face as I finally look at him.

"Nice."

He furrows his brow at my amused tone. "What?"

I poke his shoulder. "Episode 34?"

He raises his eyes to the ceiling and smirks. "Yeah. I think you're right. I didn't mean to steal the line, though. I meant it."

I laugh and he smiles with me.

"I still can't believe you remember all of it."

"I don't have amnesia. And it hasn't been that long."

He nods. "Feels like it has though."

There he goes, sucking the fun out of the conversation again. I try to bring it back. "How was the documentary?"

"You really want to know? You did dive out my window to avoid it."

Crap. Why do I fall so easily into Geek Zoe around him?

"No. Just trying small talk," I lie.

He takes a deep breath, and starts picking at a hole in his jeans. "I'd much rather hear about... you."

"What do you mean?"

"You know that thing I walked in on? Did it contribute to your bad week?"

Yes, but I'm so not talking about it. "No."

Yikes! I didn't mean to sound so rude. Like, we were totally having a good time and I snap at him.

He leans back, his eyes a bit wide. "S-sorry. It's none of my business."

What the heck? It's totally his business! I mean, *he* stopped Cody from... going further. I barked down *his* throat afterward. And he doesn't look down on me because of it. He *worries* about me.

Why *does* he worry about me? It doesn't make any sense! I ditched him. Kicked him right out of my life and kept him far from me so I wouldn't have to endure High School Emotional Hell.

And it's worked, for the most part.

Then Cody attacked me, and I've tried all my mightiest to forget about it.

But I haven't forgotten.

At all.

And I haven't talked to anyone either.

Tears prick the edges of my eyes, and I blink them back. No, no, no. I'm not going to cry, dang it. I will get through this without crying. That will make it seem like I've made a mistake by being Popular Zoe. Which I haven't.

Right?

Taking a large gulp to rid my mouth of the building saliva, I huff out a barely audible response. "What you saw with Cody... it's not usually like that."

His neck turns toward me so fast I think his head may spin off. "What do you mean?" His tone is soft, soothing, full of concern. You know, all those emotions I don't deserve.

"If you hadn't come over, he would have... I'm pretty sure he was gonna..." Something in my voice box shuts down and I can't keep going.

He leans forward, face inches away from mine. If he wants me to talk, this won't help. I can barely concentrate with him so close.

"Why did you lie to me?"

I shrug.

"Zoe." He puts his hands on mine. His skin feels so good and my inhibitions about everything, all of it, disappear. I *want* to talk to *him*. One-hundred percent as myself.

A shaky breath escapes my lips before I answer. "I was scared." Oh gosh. Here comes the flood. I turn my face from him so he doesn't see it starting. How can I explain what's going through my mind? How can I tell him without crying? How...? Just... how?

"And I-I deserved it."

His mouth pops open. "What did you say?"

"I said I was scared." I know what he means, but I don't want to repeat myself.

He leans back, letting go of my hands and kneading his forehead. "Tell me why you think you deserve to be sexually harassed."

Honesty, Zoe.

"Because I'm a slut." Because I let people believe I'm a slut. Cody probably thought I'd lead him straight to the vault, and when I didn't—

"No you're not." His face flushes, like he shot off a comment without thinking. I raise my eyebrows. "I mean... I don't think..."

My heart flutters as he tries to find the words. I let him off the hook because really, he's giving me a lot more than he knows. And I'm being stupid anyway.

"Thank you."

"For?"

I blink like crazy, trying to keep those cursed tears back, but I'm not successful. I'm crying, dang it. And I can't stop. "For thinking more of me than I'm worth."

Zak wipes my cheeks, which isn't helping because I don't freaking deserve his concern right now. So I cry harder.

"I'm sorry this happened to you," he says, shaking as he goes to tuck a piece of my hair behind my ear, but can't seem to get it right. I chuckle and he moves his hand to wipe the tears from my face again. I'm glad the shifter is between us. I think I'm about to lose it and crawl into his arms. I can't do that without wanting more from him.

He drops his hand. "No matter what you think, you don't deserve it."

I open my mouth to argue but he cuts me off. "You. Don't. Deserve. It."

I nod, even though he's only half right. I don't deserve to be attacked, but Popular Zoe signed up for this reputation. That's the price I pay for feeling accepted.

My tears turn to sniffles and Zak leans back. My body aches without him holding onto me and my bottom lip almost juts out.

Come back please. Just hold me a little longer.

The silence stretches between us, but it's not awkward. I feel relieved, like I'm finally being myself for the first time in a long time. A breath of fresh air, a weight off my shoulders, and all those other good-feeling clichés.

He gulps and wipes his palms on his jeans. "You ready to get going?"

I sigh and look at the clock. It's getting close to dinner, and I know Zak needs to get home, but I really don't want him to.

"I guess."

He chuckles. "Unless you want to grab something to eat?"

I want to. I really do. I want to sit with him and talk. Catch up, find out more about his life now, and talk Spiderman, Star Trek, Call of Duty, and everything else under the geeky sun. Maybe come up with a few kick-ass quantum theories.

But I can't risk being seen with him. What would people think? I wish I could openly date him, or at least try, because I have no idea how deep his feelings go for me, especially after all the crap I've pulled. But I'm too terrified of high school becoming middle school all over again. Besides, Zak deserves someone way better than me. I can only imagine the swirling gossip, and especially since the conversation I had with Keira today, the repercussions of going out with him would chop the head off my social status. That shouldn't be what I'm concerned about when I'm with him. But just thinking about it all makes my heart kick-start into a fury and my breathing become freaky erratic.

Calm down, Zoe.

"No. You told your mom you'd be home for dinner. You don't want to piss her off."

"Then come over and eat." He smirks at me and I roll my eyes. Another escape from the bathroom is not what I had in mind for tonight.

"Thanks, but I really should go home."

"Okay. But you're missing out on some good food."

I'm sure I am. Mrs. Gibbons's cooking is amazing from what I remember. But this whole thing has gone on long enough. Time to get back to the real world.

I turn the key, and smack my hand on the shifter. Zak buckles back up and sits there watching my arm as I try to shift.

"Um, hello?" I say giving up and waving my hand in front of him. "I still need your help."

He laughs and laces his fingers with mine over the gearbox. "Just remember, I can't hold your hand every time."

But he gives me a little squeeze, letting me know he won't mind if I ask him again.

Chapter 10

I can totally handle two personalities.

Oh. My. Gosh. That was one of the best afternoons of my life. Yes, I stalled the car about fifty times. Yes, I talked about my nasty ex-boyfriend. Yes, I bawled my eyes dry. But I can't stop smiling. I thought I couldn't like that nerdboy any more than I already did, but all the scrunched up queasy feelings turned into a riot in my belly the second he put his hand on mine.

Boy, am I in trouble.

And I'm totally on a high! I want to scream it out to someone. Dance around and squeal and do all that stuff girls do with their girlfriends when they meet THE guy. It totally sucks 'cause I can't.

But I want to talk boys. Just to get it out. Make it official that I'm totally into him and then maybe I can push it away forever.

I blow up my cheeks and pull my laptop out.

All I have to do is show a little bit of control. I don't have to go all-out nerd with Hope. Just tell her I'm into a guy and like, it's totally awesome. Then she can squeal and show the proper enthusiasm without actually knowing who it is.

I can do this.

No problem.

I log on and see Hope's online. Sweet! I open a chat window and start typing.

Zoester: Hey girl!

Hopin4lovin: hi! What you up to?

Zoester: Nothing. Just got home.

Hopin4lovin: From where? I thought you were grounded?

Zoester: From my old friends. Not from new ones. ;)

Hopin4lovin: OMG! spill!

Zoester: Not much to tell. ;)

Hopin4lovin: Come on! Tell me!

Zoester: Just a guy.

Hopin4lovin: Who????

Zoester: No one you know. But he's amazing!

Hopin4lovin: Not gonna tell me? Zoe, I'm your best bud!

Zoester: I know. I wanna see where it's going first.

Hopin4lovin: Gotcha. Glad you're in a better mood.

Zoester: Me too.

See, totally can handle this. I tell Hope a quick g'nite and shut off the computer. Since I'm "grounded" I probably shouldn't be using it a lot anyway. It'll help Geek Control too.

I'm still smiling as I dress for bed. When I shimmy off my tight jeans and low cut blouse, it's only then I realize Zak's eyes never lingered over my body. At least, not that I noticed. He always kept his gaze locked on my face, or my hands. Maybe that's why things are so different with him. He's not constantly ogling me.

Wait a minute. Maybe he doesn't think I'm attractive enough to ogle. I run to the full length mirror. I'm only in my underwear, but it gives me the opportunity to assess everything.

I guess I'm a little too curvy. I have some love handles, but all girls have those right? Except those freaky skinny ones. My hair still looks hot even though some of the color rinsed out in the shower. I've always been proud of my boobs, but maybe it's the bra making them look so big and perky.

I cringe as I adjust myself, trying to see if I fill the underwear properly. After a few minutes of tugging at it, I huff and slink my arms down to my sides, smacking my hips.

Agh! My hips are so wide! And I have thunder thighs.

I bring my arm up and play with the sagging fat by my armpit. I've heard all girls have this too, but mine is nasty. How did I ever think I was hot?

Zak's phone rings, which jolts me out of my boob dancing and fat flailing. It's his house phone, and the answering machine picks up right away, which I can hear loud and clear. Mrs. Gibbons's sweet voice echoes through the open window.

You've reached Maddie and Zak. Leave a message and we'll get back to you when we can. BEEP.

There's silence for a brief moment, and I figure whoever it is decided to hang up, but then a deep voice, one I haven't heard in over three years, stammers from the line.

Hi Zak. I-It's Dad. Just wanted to see h-how you were. You know school and stuff.

Dad?! I must've heard that wrong. I stick my head out my

window so my ears don't lie to me again. No way is Zak's dad calling him.

Um, if you get this before tomorrow, I'm gonna be at the Econo Lodge in Sante Fe. Room 25, so if you want to call me back, that's where I'll be.

He pauses.

So, yeah. I guess I'll…

Another pause.

L-love you son. CLICK.

Oh shit. Shit, shit, shit. Zak can *not* hear that message. After years of silence, Zak wrote his dad off, and this? It would destroy him. And even thinking about the effect it'll have on his mom makes me shudder.

What do I do? I mean, I could rush over and delete the dang thing before Zak gets home. I don't know where the crap he is, or how long he'll be gone, but I know where his hide-a-key is. I can be quick.

Or should I even worry about it? He's not my friend, right? I mean, not in public.

Agh! What the hell do I do?!

I know what I should do. Get that message off his phone. It's totally meddling, but I can't even imagine the look on his face if he hears it. I don't want to see him lose it like I lost it today. I don't want to see him in that much pain. Especially if I can prevent it.

I pull on my "Mr. Hyde" sweatshirt which couldn't be more ironic with all my mood swings today, and a light from Zak's driveway catches my eye.

Dammit! He's home!

Forget the hide-a-key. Forget the front door altogether. I gotta get over there stat! I take a deep breath and a few steps back from the window. I haven't done this in so long, I hope I'm still capable without getting hurt.

I launch myself outside, hooking my hands on Zak's window ledge.

Yikes! At least I didn't miss.

I pull up slowly—thank you fourth period gym!—and a sliver digs itself into my thigh.

Holy crap, that hurt!

I hop into his room, ignoring the throbbing from the dang sliver and try not to breathe in too much because of how distracted Zak's amazing scent would make me. I cross over to the answering machine which I'm so glad is in his room in the first place and I don't have to book it to the kitchen.

Oh gosh, how do I work this thing?

Right as I find the delete button, Zak's door swings open.

Chapter 11

Who knew pulling out a sliver could be so sexy?

"You know, I think I'm going to ask Mom to start locking the door when we leave. We don't want any crazy neighbors to get in." He chuckles and shrugs out of his jacket.

My back hovers over the machine, and I hope he won't immediately go to it. My fingers are slipping over buttons, but I'm afraid I'll accidentally hit PLAY instead, so I don't push anything. "Um, I came through the window."

He shakes his head, letting his hair wave away from his eyes. He's laughing as he peeks outside. "Did you lose your pants?"

Gah! How could I forget I'm only in a sweatshirt and underwear? I want to act cool, like it's totally on purpose. I mean, I do that all the time! I prance around in much less, but I find myself grabbing his blanket and awkwardly wrapping it around me.

"Sorry," I mumble. "I forgot to put them on." Could things get any worse?

He pulls out a pair of jeans and tosses them at me, his face lobster red. "Well, wear these till you remember yours."

My jittery hands do not help as I pull up his pants, which are too big. I suck a breath through my teeth as the material scrapes against that darn sliver.

"Did you hurt yourself?" His amusement wipes from his voice, replaced with that worried look I still don't know why he gives me.

"It's nothing. Don't worry about it."

"You sure?"

"Just a sliver."

He gulps and for the first time I see his eyes flicker to my legs and stay there.

"You should really get it out before it gets infected." His voice and hands shake, and his face flushes so dark, steam would come off him if I poured water over his head.

Maybe my thighs aren't as thunderous as I thought. I smile, and let the jeans fall to the ground, stepping out of them gently while keeping my eyes locked on him.

"Will you help me?" My heart crashes around my chest. I've done the whole sexy, flirty thing millions of times, but I never meant it. I'm not using Zak for anything. I just want him to find Geek Zoe sexy. To totally treat me like I'm his own Princess Leia.

He closes his eyes and turns his back on me. I'm ready for a rejection, for him to tell me to go home, but instead he grabs a pair of tweezers from his desk and motions for me to sit on the bed.

He sits next to me, his eyes desperately trying not to look at my bare skin, but I know he has to. *He* knows he has to, but he's fighting it.

I should help him out, even though he's being so cute, and I like seeing him get all nervous because of… *me*. The sliver is jammed into my inner thigh, high enough you can see my cute boy short underwear—good thing I didn't go with the thong today—but low enough he won't have to touch my crotch. I pull up the oversized sweatshirt so it reveals more of my attire, but I stick my leg out in such an unsexy way I'm sure he'll be able to control his shaking hands.

He laughs as I almost kick him in the face, and he moves to the floor, crouching so he can get a better look at the nasty thing.

"Ouch. I wouldn't call this much of a sliver. More of a twig."

I punch him in the shoulder. "Well, maybe you should consider sanding down your ledge."

"I didn't realize my neighbor would leap into my room in her underwear."

"Ha ha."

The cold tip of the tweezers hits my burning leg, and I cringe.

"Does it hurt?"

"No. Just cold."

"Try to hold still. I don't want to hurt you." His voice hitches on the last sentence, and I suppress the wide smile that wants to form on my lips. Holding still is going to be a problem.

We're silent as he tries to get it out. I wince from the brief seconds of pain, but mostly I focus on the way he keeps his distance. Like he doesn't *want* to touch me. I know this'll go a lot faster if he grabs my leg to balance while he works, but he doesn't. The only touch I feel is from the tweezers.

But there's a tension in the air I can't ignore. Our stuttered breathing patterns, the heat radiating off our bodies, the building sweat on his forehead, and the pounding my heart makes in my ears. Goosebumps erupt over my skin, like it's trying to reach out and close the distance between his fingers and my leg.

I close my eyes and hold my breath. My hands clench around the pillow on his bed as I fight every urge to knock the stupid tweezers out of the way and tackle him to the floor.

"There."

The air I've been holding flutters out in small wisps as I look at the giant sliver he pulled from my leg.

"Thank you."

"No problem." He pats my leg as he stands. Then as if he's forgotten he's avoiding touching me, he jerks his hand back and hides his face.

I tuck my legs back together, smiling at his reaction. Standing, I tug the sweatshirt down so he doesn't see my underwear. I don't want to make him uncomfortable.

"So, uh," he stutters, "why are you in my room?" He's still not looking at me as he crosses to the desk to put the tweezers away.

"Oh, well, um." Great. Now I'm the one stuttering. I'd completely forgotten why I flew myself across our houses with the temporary distraction, but now it zaps back to my head. My eyes flicker to the blinking light on the machine right as he turns around.

"Zoe," he says smirking, "did you leave an embarrassing message on my phone?"

Crap.

Before I can move to delete the darn thing, he bolts past me, reaching for the play button.

I jump on his back, making him lose his balance and smack into the floor. I straddle him, pinning his arms down with my knees. He's laughing hysterically, but stops when he hears the dreaded voice I can't stop in time.

"Hi Zak. I-It's Dad."

His smile fades, and his mouth opens wide. He's staring right into my face, but I know he's not really looking at me. He's listening to every word on that message. And with each word, his eyes shine more and more with tears he's forcing back.

This is the face I didn't want to see. The pain and shock and just… everything I can't make better. I don't know how. I just don't want to see this look on his face ever again.

We don't relax after the message ends. We sit in a tense silence, me still on top of him.

What do I say? What do I say?!

"Are… are you okay?" I know it's a dumb question, but it's the only thing in my head.

He nods, but it's too rapid to be the truth. I take my knees off him, and sit to his side. He still doesn't move.

I don't know what to do. Or if I'm even the right person to do it. He's just lying there, staring at the ceiling with that horrid expression still glued on his face.

Come on, Zoe. You used to be good at this stuff. Especially when it came to him.

Because nothing else comes to mind, I grasp his hand, which seems to bring him back to life. He stares at it, his brow furrowing,

CASSIE MAE

like I've suddenly grown fur or something.

Maybe that wasn't the thing to do.

But he pulls me down on the floor and holds me against his side.

A few minutes ago, this would've made me incredibly happy. To lie here in his arms and feel his warm body against mine, but right now I feel sad for him. I rub his chest, and he holds my hand there.

"I'm sorry," I whisper into his armpit. He squeezes me tighter, still not saying anything. I reach for the blanket I dropped on the floor earlier with my toes and pull it up over us. He lets me use his arm as a pillow, and I trace the words on his T-shirt, which I didn't notice until now, say Dr. Jekyll.

Finally, after almost an hour, he says something.

"You awake?"

I look up to see his face, but his eyes are closed. I nod and snuggle into him more.

"I never thought I'd hear his voice again," he says over my head. "When he left, I thought he'd be gone for good."

Now I'm the one who doesn't say anything. I can't think of the last time Zak talked about his dad. And that's not because we've had a falling out. Ever since his dad left, it was a forbidden topic. Like saying Voldemort.

"You heard the message didn't you? That's why you risked your neck to get in here?"

"Uh… yeah."

He pulls my chin up so I can look into his dark, watery eyes. "I didn't know I could count on you like that."

Something inside me whips around like beaters mixing cookie dough. I'm suddenly aware of how vulnerable I've become with him. How I want to melt into him. How much I want him to kiss me and never stop. And maybe I could keep it all a secret. Hide it from everyone at school. From my friends. From my family. From everyone.

But I can't do that to him. He deserves more than that. More than me.

I want to shove my insecurities away. Make them all disappear somehow, but I can't find the strength. Half of me gets excited envisioning his hand around mine as we walk down the halls at school, but the other half starts hyperventilating to the point of getting sick.

And then everything else shoves itself into my mind. How high school will become middle school all over again.

The whispers.

The shouted insults.

The disgusted looks from people I thought were my friends.

The desperate attempts to be liked for who I really am, and failing.

Crying over the gossip.

Crying over the hurt feelings.

Crying over everything. Just because of what I like. Of *who* I like.

It's better to pretend. It's better to be fake because it hurts less.

I shrug out of his arms and swipe my cheeks before Zak can see. He sits up and watches as I strip the blanket off and walk to the window.

"You should probably take the stairs." His voice sounds defeated, but it's probably more due to his dad than me. Though he knows what goes through my head most of the time, I doubt he knows how screwed up I am.

"I'm not supposed to be out this late. I don't want to get caught."

"I don't want you to get hurt." He glances at the clock. "And your parents aren't home yet. Just hurry."

He's right, and I'm trying to ignore he knows this much about me and my family still. I get to the door, resting my hand on the knob.

"You'll be okay, right?" I ask.

"Yes."

I pause, blowing up my cheeks.

"What's wrong?" he asks, slowly getting to his feet.

"I worry about you."

He smirks—that beautiful smile that plays my heart strings like a harp. "Do you… I mean, are you up for another driving lesson tomorrow?"

"I thought you worked on Tuesdays." Again my mouth shoots off before I can control it. If he realizes how much I know about him he's going to think I'm a stalker.

"Not this week."

"Oh."

He chuckles as he waits for me to answer, but my mind isn't focused on what he's saying.

"Zoe?"

"Um, yeah. Tomorrow's fine."

He nods, and I turn back around to open the door.

"Hey," Zak says, stopping me again.

"Hmm?"

"Will you not tell my mom about this?"

I force a smile. "Mum's the word."

"And here." He tosses his jeans at me. "Please don't run across the street without pants on."

Chapter 12

I'm a horrible human being.

I'm so glad I closed my window last night because I probably made some very embarrassing noises in my sleep. I blame his jeans being stuffed in my face while I slept. Yes, I'm that big of a fool to sleep with them like a teddy bear.

Stretching out on the bed, I pick up my phone, which is blinking at me with about twenty messages.

The first few are from Keira, asking me if I hooked up with Levi yesterday since she couldn't get a hold of me. Then—speak of the devil—there's about ten from Levi, who's carrying on a conversation with himself apparently, because I didn't text back.

The last message scrolls up, which I assume is Levi again, but my stomach lurches when I see Zak's name.

Thanks.

Oh boy. I can't tell if I'm happy or sad or angry or frustrated or relieved or guilty. I'm torn so many places I can't put my head on straight.

What have I done? It's okay for *me* to have nerdy fantasies. But he can't latch onto me. I'm no good for him.

I set my phone back on the nightstand without replying and chuck Zak's jeans across the room, pissed at myself for letting my guard down. It's not like my poor attempt at deleting that message from his dad was at all successful. I should've let it go.

But thinking of his face as he heard his dad's voice made me happy he wasn't alone, even if he had to be with a fake bitch like me.

Getting dressed poses a dilemma. For some bizarre reason, I feel like more of a dirty whore than usual as I tug on tight jeans and corseted top. Very cute and sexy, and really pushing the dress code boundaries with the bursting cleavage.

And so not me today.

But it *has* to be me today.

I shrug on my leather jacket, whipping my hair out so it flows down my back. Sighing, I grab my purse and Chemistry book, and zip out the door.

Walking to school in heels sucks butt. Hope's been giving me rides, but she's late most of the time, and I really can't miss any more classes.

The hallway's buzzing by the time I get to school and as usual it's almost impossible to fit in the student union. As I slide between two tall guys I see some people over by the vending machines, doing replays of the last football game. Josh plows into Tyler's side while the girls squeal. I roll my eyes which land on the "loners" chipping at their black nail polish. That stuff is so hard to get off. Especially the glitter kind. I'd ask them what their secret is, but again…they're out of my social league.

A few people play bad guitar for a "pretending to be interested" crowd. And Keira sits in the midst of four guys, flirting away as she lightly touches her cleavage, strokes their arms, and giggles at their probably less than funny, inappropriate comments.

I make my way over, really trying not to pout and knowing if I don't walk over there people will wonder what's wrong with me. Three of the four guys surrounding Keira gravitate in my direction as I walk up.

Geek Zoe, you have to leave now.

"Lookin' hot," Jesse says, eyes locked on my boobs. Makes me wonder if he's talking to me or them.

BJ throws an arm over my shoulders and slaps a kiss on my cheek.

Yup, life seems to have gone on just fine even though I felt like I was in another world yesterday. I smile at the attention I'm getting by simply walking in the door. "Hi Zoe!" and "Sup girl?" and, just like Jesse, "Lookin' hot!" phrases are sent my way.

I'm ready to pull out from under BJ's arm, but I remember Popular Zoe would stay there. Obviously the breakup between me and Cody has made its official rounds, and since I threw myself at Levi so quickly, I'm sure the word "loose" has my picture next to it in the social dictionary. If it didn't already.

Hunter keeps his distance, though he walked over with the other two boys. His eyes graze the crown of my head to my glittery toenails with a questioning look. I tug at my corset and my boobs almost pop out.

"What?"

He shakes his head and mumbles, "Oh, hi."

I'm about to ask him what that look was for, but Keira interrupts my thoughts.

"Hey Zoe." Keira's voice has a bite to it, like I purposely tried to steal the attention.

"Hey."

"I heard you and Cody split." Jesse runs his hand through his hair and smiles like he's waiting for me to throw myself at him.

Subtle.

"Yeah."

"D'ya know what he's been sayin'?" BJ cocks an eyebrow at me, but it's not nearly as sexy as when Zak does it.

"No. And I don't care." I sit down on the carpeted steps next to Keira, and she hands me a granola bar.

Hunter keeps his lips pressed tight together, still looking at me like I have the plague. BJ shuffles his feet before nudging Keira's shoe.

"What?" she nearly shrieks at him. "If she doesn't care, then she doesn't need to know."

Taking my time, I study each of their faces. The guys all look like lost puppies, and Keira looks almost bored.

I groan. "Fine. What did he say?"

No one answers. Gosh, what the hell is so bad? If he said I didn't put out, that's not so bad, but if he made up a lie, which sounds more like him, I'm not sure what to expect.

I nudge Keira a little too hard in the arm.

"Ow. Geez. He just said you gave him Chlamydia."

"What?!" I bark out laughing. "He's insane."

"So it's not true?" Hunter asks, perking right up.

"Hell no."

The small group breathes a collective sigh. Hunter actually slides between me and Keira, setting his hand dangerously close to my butt. I allow it, though I feel like smacking him across the face.

Sure, they give Popular Zoe a chance to explain herself. They give her the time of day when rumors fly around about her. But the second they find out Popular Zoe is actually Geek Zoe in disguise they'll all laugh at her.

"I knew he was full of shit." Keira reaches over Hunter to pat my knee, but I can see her real intention is to give Hunter a better boob shot.

"Well, if he has Chlamydia, he didn't get it from me."

"You going to go get tested then?"

I shake my head. "No need. We didn't get that far."

It was like I said some dirty word with the way the boys stare at me. Hunter drops his hand from my waist and recoils. BJ gawks like an idiot and Jesse's eyes finally leave my boobs and rest on my own, waiting for a punch line or something.

Only Keira rolls her eyes. "Yeah, o-kay."

I let it go. No point in arguing with people who won't believe me anyway. Hope would back me up, but darn girl is late. The boys relax again after I don't say anything, either assuming I was only joking, or because Keira moved on to a more interesting subject, I don't know. But I'm not sure if I care either. My mind's not in the conversation. Soon the first bell rings and people scurry off to class.

I pull my purse back over my shoulder and snug my chemistry book to my chest. I have to get to my locker before first period, but Hunter will not let go of me.

"I'll walk you to class," he says, tucking his hand into my back pocket. Guess he couldn't help himself this time.

He leads me to my locker, hand firmly on my butt cheek the whole way. I feel sick, and I'm ready to slug him, but the envious stares I receive make me hold back.

Popular Zoe would want this. Hunter is *hot*. He's been lip locked with the same girl for about a year, but since Lindsay cheated on him last week, he's fresh on the market. Probably looking for someone to make him forget.

And it's obvious who his choice is.

A smile creeps onto my face again as I realize exactly how awesome I am at this stuff. Guys want *me*. Girls want to be *me*.

Well, fake me. But I can't think like that.

Bending down at my locker to swap books, I'm finally released from his grasp. He leans against the other lockers as he waits for me.

"Hey Zo."

Ah. Only one person calls me Zo. And now my stomach is in my butt.

Zak shuffles his feet on the other side of me, the locker door separating us. My face probably looks like the inside of a toaster. I can't talk to him in front of Hunter. But I don't want to hurt him either.

I suck in a deep breath through my nostrils. "Uh, hi." Crap, my voice is shaking. I need to sound confident. I need to sound, I don't know, like I'm not crazy about him.

My eyes flicker to Hunter's face who is suppressing a giant laugh.

Oh gosh. *Breathe, Zoe.*

"I, um, wanted to know if…" Zak stops. I close my locker and try to paste a mask on. Anything that'll make Hunter not look at me like I've got poop smeared all over my face.

"Wanted to know what?" Argh. I hate this. I can tell I'm hurting Zak by the way he's staring at me. And Hunter scoots closer, snuggling in the curve of my shoulder.

I feel like such a bitch.

Zak's eyes zap between me and horny boy. He slides his tongue over his lips before continuing. "I wanted to know if you needed a ride home today."

Hunter moves his head from my neck and looks at me, eyebrows raised and mouth hanging open.

I can't blow up my cheeks now. I want to. I'm *really* trying not to. But I'm in major panic mode. He's going to tell everyone I'm talking with my geeky next door neighbor. He's going to tell them I need a ride from the boy who's an active player at the D&D table.

Then the real gossip will begin.

The truth might get out.

Oh gosh.

"Look Zak," I stumble over the name, like I'm not sure if it's right, "this is starting to get really sad." Hunter laughs, but it doesn't make me feel better. I'm almost in tears as I go from fake bitch, to real life bitch. "A piece of advice, get a new hobby. Stalking isn't working."

The words are out and the look on Zak's face is the same one as last night. The one I never wanted to see again. Hunter tugs me to first period, jamming his hand in my back pocket before either me or Zak can say anything else.

I don't look over my shoulder. I can't. Think of all the bitchy words in existence, and they don't even come close to describing me.

I'm crying now, but Hunter doesn't even notice. His eyes are locked on my boobs. By the time I get to my class, I've wiped my face clean.

"Thanks. I can take it from here," I say as I pull the door open to Ms. Weber's classroom. I can't help but think if Zak was here, and if I hadn't just stabbed him in the gut, he'd open the door for me, without going all cross-eyed at my exploding bosoms.

On the walk home, I seriously wish I wasn't so insecure. Zak's face won't leave my head, and I spent all day either looking for him or avoiding him depending on who I was with. I even drafted up a few text messages. Logged on FB and sent some IMs. But I did it all in the stalls of the girls' bathroom. Or I made sure no one was looking over my shoulder in the library. How can I say "Whoops! Sorry about that whole stalker thing" when I'm still doing the same shit? So I never sent the messages.

I'm a freaking horrible person, I know.

And I really could've used a ride since Hope bailed on me. I take off my heels as soon as I hit the sidewalk of my street. The muscles in my feet send up their gratitude and the first real smile I've had today soaks my expression.

I hate rule three.

My house is empty. Seirra's not home from school yet, since she gets out later than me. Charter schools. Bleck. I'm glad my parents didn't force me into one.

Mom and Dad are working. Always working.

There's a note on the counter telling me dinner's made and in the fridge whenever we get hungry. Also a "friendly" reminder that Sierra's butt is grounded, and I have to make sure she stays home.

I slink upstairs, still feeling like banging my face on the walls. I really hate myself today.

I mean, I hate myself most days. But today…

Yeah. I suck.

I try to rationalize the stupid reactions I have when I'm at school. Telling myself I only acted that way to Zak because he can't fall for someone like me, but that's a big ass lie.

I'm not who I used to be. Not really. Zak should know that. He's been a witness to it since we started high school. If he keeps bugging me it's his own fault.

But he's not bugging me. *I* asked him to teach me to drive. *I* played four hours of Lord of the Rings with him. *I* leapt the distance between our windows so I could stop that voicemail.

And it's me who can't seem to get past my insecurities. The desire to have the attention, to be liked and popular, keeps me from being myself.

Popular Zoe needs to go to sleep now. I'm tired of her.

I look down at my corset. The stupid thing keeps digging into my sides. I yank the snaps open and chuck it across the room. Finding the most boring bra I own, I pull it on, then cover my top half with my Harry Potter shirt.

The comforter on the bed still smells like Zak's cologne, so when I toss it over my head, all the pain I try to escape intensifies.

There aren't words harsh enough to describe how evil I am.

I *have* to make it up to him. Not just because his douche of a father called last night. Because he's my...

I gulp.

Friend.

Or at least, I want him to be.

I think.

No.

I know.

I *do* want him to be my friend again. Not just because I like who I am with him, but because no matter how awful I've been to him, he's always been the opposite to me.

Chapter 13

Why do I try to make things better? I suck at it.

I pull on a bright pink hoodie to cover my shirt. I'm still wearing my tight jeans, so no worries this time about going over in just my underwear.

Snatching his pants off the floor, I peek out the window to see if his is open.

It's not.

Darn it. Guess I'll have to go over the traditional way, even if that means getting a door slammed in my face.

After knocking, I shove my hands into the front pocket of my sweater. I think there's a sensor or something on his porch that increases heart rates. My pulse beats out of my neck.

Mrs. Gibbons answers, wearing her security uniform.

"Zoe!"

"Hi Maddie."

"Come in, please."

The smell of pumpkin spice tickles my nostrils and sends waves of memories into my brain when I get inside. Mrs. Gibbons makes the best pumpkin cheesecake.

"Two days in a row," she says her eyes beaming. "I take it you're reconnecting with my little Zakary?"

Am I that transparent? Is "I'm friends with a sexy nerd" written all over my body? I attempt one of those half smiles Zak does, but I feel a little queasy.

"You know…" She pulls me under her arm and taps a finger across my nose. "I used to be envious of you two."

My eyebrows shoot upward and I wish she'd pull back. Nothing like a fresh wave of guilt to top off the nausea.

"I never had a friend who lived so close to me. Well, at least one I had so much in common with."

She squeezes my shoulders.

"Zak is lucky he has someone like you to talk to."

There goes my stomach falling into my butt again. Yeah, he's sure lucky to have someone like me. Someone who will hop into his room when no one is around, but the second she senses someone laughing at her for talking with him, she calls him a stalker and tells him to leave her alone. I'm a real good buddy.

"Um…" Yeah, that's all I can get to come out my mouth. Maybe puke if she keeps talking.

She giggles as she leaves my personal bubble. "I'll go get him."

She doesn't yell up the stairs like normal moms do. She actually goes and gets him. I take another big inhale, letting the spice fill my nostrils. Ah, I miss this house. I miss feeling comfortable here. If it was back in the day, I wouldn't have even used the door. Zak's window would've been open, and I'd impress him with my ninja window jumping skills, challenge him to a two-hour Doctor Who trivia session, and any fight we may have just had would be long forgotten. I shuffle my feet in the entryway, trying to shut off the thing in my nose that allows me to smell. But that just makes me sneeze.

"Bless you."

Zak takes his time going down the stairs, like he's afraid I'm going to suddenly bite him or something.

Yeah, I don't blame him.

"Thanks."

"What do you want?"

He seems to ask that a lot. And I never give him an honest answer.

"Uh, here," I say, holding his jeans out.

He cocks his eyebrow in that awesome sexy way and takes them.

"You washed them already?"

Crap. "No, sorry."

He shrugs and tosses them down the hall toward the laundry room.

"That all?" He tucks his hands in his back pockets, his plaid overshirt opening to reveal his Team Fred and George T-shirt.

My mouth fires off without me thinking. "Did you wear that shirt to school today?"

"Yeah." He pulls his hands out of his pockets and folds his arms, covering the words. "Is that all you want?"

Throwing him a sheepish grin, I pull up my hoodie so he can see my shirt. I'm ready for his mouth to upturn in that irresistible smile, but instead he goes blood-orange red and tugs my sweater back down.

"If you don't need anything else, I've got a lot of stuff to do."

"Zak, I..."

"You can save it."

I startle back from his tone. "Save what?"

"Whatever you want to say. It doesn't matter."

"Why do you say that?" I'm trying to keep the hurt out of my voice, but I don't know how successful I am.

He glares at me, like I should be smart enough to figure it out. "I really do have a lot of crap to do." He rubs his eyes with his forefinger and thumb. "So, if that's all you want, you should go."

"I-I'm sorry," I sputter.

He shakes his head. "I don't want to hear it, Zo."

I'm chipping at him. He used the nickname.

"It's not like that with me and Hunter. I... he wanted... I can't..." Argh! I can't get the words out because I don't know what the right ones are.

"You think I'm upset because some guy was all over you?"

I nod—lying to him. Again. I know it's much deeper than that.

"Guys are always all over you. At least the ones you talk to."

I'm not sure what to say. He's right, so I can't argue. So I say the only thing I can. "I'm sorry."

He sighs, dropping his hands back into his pockets. "Don't worry about it. Like I said yesterday, it's not like we're friends or anything."

I really wish he'd stop saying that.

"Will you still give me a driving lesson today?" I know I'm pushing his limits. But I can't help myself. I want to spend time with him. I have to do something to clean up the mess I made, even though I'll probably end up making it worse.

But it's like I'm addicted to him or something.

"I don't know."

I gulp, and dig up the courage to say something I haven't in a long time. "Please?"

Zak raises his eyebrow again, probably surprised I asked nicely. He seems to argue with himself, chomping his teeth and running his hands through his feathery hair, interlocking his fingers behind his neck. I play with my ring underneath the pocket of my hoodie, trying really hard not to blow out my cheeks as I wait.

Finally he opens the door and steps outside. "Let's go. But it's gonna be a short lesson today."

I nod, forcing back the wide smile that wants to glue itself on my face as I follow him to my car. "Thanks."

Zak doesn't open my door for me, but it sure looks like he wants to. He stops halfway up the drive and stares at the car like it's giving him a pop quiz. Then he slumps his shoulders and climbs into the passenger seat.

Guess I'm not as forgiven as I thought.

I strap the seatbelt on, my hands shaking like the paint mixer again. Zak's not paying attention to me though. He's picking at the stray fabric on his holey jeans, not a word passing his lips.

"Okay, so I just need to keep my foot on the clutch and the brake to start the car?" I ask, trying to lighten the tension in the air.

He nods.

A defeated sigh seeps out as I turn the key. He doesn't offer to shift. Still says nothing as I smack my hand on the stick, shoving it downward into that screwed up reverse position. The only response I get is his eyebrows shooting skyward in approval.

He starts picking at his jeans again as I back up.

And stall.

I growl and let my head fall on the steering wheel. "Are you sure you want to do this?"

"Are you talking to yourself, or me?"

I puff up my cheeks and let it out before I answer. "You."

"Look, I said I'd teach you how. So I'm going to follow through."

"But you don't want to." I peek under my arm so I can get a look at his face. He presses his wrist in between his eyebrows, like he's got a major headache or something.

"Just start the car, Zo."

I want to cry. I totally deserve the frosty attitude, but it doesn't mean it hurts any less. Zak's only been this pissed at me once. And it was my fault then too.

Instead of apologizing again, since it'd be pointless, I start the car, put it in gear and try to stay calm as I reverse out of the driveway. When I get to the street, I'm not sure how to shift, but I try my best, Zak watching my hand without making a sound.

The grinding the car makes as I shove the shifter in first makes me cringe, but Zak still stays silent. He doesn't look bored, or annoyed, or even angry. He looks like he's beyond caring. I'd rather take the anger.

The car jerks forward as I ease off the throttle, rocking us both in our seats. This continues during the entire drive to the parking lot we went to before. I pull in, and shut off the car, my eyes watering. I can't tell if I'm more humiliated or hurt because of what I've done to him.

"You did really good." His voice still sounds like he's trying not to care, but he's saying it anyway. "It takes practice."

I nod, 'cause my voice will totally come out all juicy and snotty if I attempt to use it.

It's silent between us, that horrid awkward silence that makes the tension in the air like sniffing glue. I feel sick, and stupid, and want it to all go away.

A growl erupts from Zak's throat which makes me recoil in my seat.

"What's wrong?" he asks.

His concern locks a fist around my throat, making me croak out my words. "What?"

"There's something wrong. What is it?"

I shake my head. "It's nothing. Just forget it."

"Zo…"

His hand goes for mine, but then he stops mid-air. A heat wave comes off his face as he pretends he was just going to scratch an imaginary itch.

"I don't like it when you're mad at me," I blurt. "Even though you have every right to be pissed."

Zak growls again. A really guttural and menacing growl as he smacks his fist on the roof of the car. "I don't get you."

"What do you mean?" I say, though I know exactly what he means. I don't get me either.

"What is this to you?" He waves his hand between the two of us. "Are you using me like you use everyone? Once you know how to drive that'll be it?"

He thinks I *use* people? Oh gosh. He's starting to think Popular Zoe is the real Zoe. I mean, that's what I thought I wanted, but it's totally not. I like that he knows Geek Zoe. Because Geek Zoe is just… Zoe.

"Do you want that to be it?"

"You're not answering me. I don't like games. So if you want this to be a teacher-student thing, then keep it that way. No more treating me the way you do at school then coming over to say sorry so I'll help you. No more jumping across our windows to get into my room. You obviously don't care as much as I thought you did."

"No, please…" I stutter, my eyes ready to flood out. Great. "I didn't mean… at school, it's just so different. I don't know what happens to me."

"I know exactly what happens to you." He shakes his head and starts clicking the light saber keychain on his hip.

"But… I… I never ever mean to… I guess I don't think about it hurting you." I slam my face on the steering wheel again. "I'm selfish. That's what happens to me. I can't think about anyone but myself when I'm there."

"I don't think that's true either."

My brow crinkles as I turn to him. "What?"

"If you only thought about yourself, who you really are, you wouldn't care about what other people think so much." He looks out his window, his breath fogging up the glass. "And you're still not answering me."

"What was the question, again?"

He rolls his head back to look at me. "Are you using me?"

I shake my head wildly. It may come off its hinges.

"You're saying you want to be my friend again?"

Is that hope in his voice? Like, does he want that too?

I totally want to be close to him. To hug him and tell him that's exactly what I want. Without really thinking, I unbuckle my seatbelt and lean over him, taking in his intoxicating scent. His breath catches with his surprise at our proximity, but he doesn't move. His eyes lock with mine, searching for the answer to his question.

A flash of movement passes the window behind his head, pulling my eyes away from his.

Outside, BJ and Keira walk across the park grass, snuggled into each other, laughing and flirting.

Crap. If they look this way and see me leaning over Zak like this, I mean forget the Chlamydia rumors. It'll all be about me seducing the Head Nerd. It sucks to think of Zak that way. Because he's so much more than just someone people make fun of. He's fun, funny, super awesome to hang out with, and accepts people for who they are. He's not afraid either. To be himself.

And I'm nothing like that.

I'm afraid of myself.

I reach over Zak and yank on the seat release and he flies back, letting out a yelp.

I fumble around with the keys, start the car and screech out of the parking lot without stalling the dang thing.

Zak adjusts his seat. "What was that about?" He turns around to look out the back window, and his voice lowers. "Oh."

I open my mouth to say the apology on my tongue, but he stops it.

"I think you've got the hang of this driving stick stuff. Take me home."

I nod, because there's really nothing to say, and then stall the car.

I try again.

And again.

And again.

Still nothing. My legs shake too much to concentrate, and all of a sudden Zak yells at me.

"You have to feather the clutch, Zoe! You're doing it too fast."

My defenses zap into place as another wave of tears splash down my cheeks. I'm always crying around him. "I'm *trying!*"

He puts his hand on my knee, but it's totally not sexy. He tries to control my foot as I let it off the clutch.

The car goes forward, then comes to an abrupt stop.

"ARRR!" I scream and shake the steering wheel. I so can't do this right now. I'm hurting him. Hurting me. Hurting everyone.

"Get out." Zak unbuckles his seatbelt and opens his door.

"What?"

"Get out!"

I crawl into the passenger seat, pouting like a freaking five-year-old. I know the person I should be pissed at is me, but Zak is the one who's going to get the brunt of it.

"I'm sorry! I can't concentrate!"

"It's 'cause you're in too much of a hurry to get out of here without being seen with me," he snaps. "So let me help you."

He starts the car and shifts like a crazy racecar driver, and before I know it, we're back in my driveway.

"Were you watching?" he says as he chucks the keys in my lap. "That's how you drive stick. And that's your last lesson. Hope you learned something."

"Zak, wait." He doesn't. He's already halfway across the lawn separating our houses by the time I catch up to him.

"Look, I'm sorry," I say grabbing his arm.

"Just stop it!" He jerks back from my hold and I stare at him like an idiot. "Why am I such an embarrassment to you?"

Again, I have no answer for him. He shakes his head, his hair flying around his face.

"Forget it."

Everything inside me says I need to go after him, but I stay put. There's nothing I can say that wouldn't be totally contradictory to what I *do*.

I stop the flow of tears and stomp to my bedroom, slamming the door so hard I'm surprised my house is still standing.

Flattening my lips into a straight line, I gaze out my window at Zak's room. He wants to chuck keys at me? Yell? Continue to be dork of the year? Fine.

He'll never understand anyway. He won't get it. He's never been popular. He's never had to hide who he really is because *he* can handle it.

I can't.

And I'll probably never be able to.

Chapter 14

Someone needs to explain to him what a booty call is.

"Will Hope's parents be home?" Dad shuts the fridge and pops open a can of Diet Coke before looking at me. I give him the "impatient daughter" roll of the eyes.

"Yes, Dad. It's just a sleepover. Girl stuff."

He takes a sip before answering. "Girl stuff." He pauses, taking another drink. "No boys then?"

Duh. "No boys, Dad. It's going to be Hope and me. Maybe Keira." That's a flat ass lie.

I haven't seen Zak since our fight, and I yell at myself every time I realize I'm thinking about it. It's not like I can make anything better... or that I want to. I'm done with that craptastic attempt at getting his attention.

Jesse's party tonight is exactly what I need to forget this whole frakking mess.

"I don't know…" Dad leans against the counter and it creaks under his weight. "Who's going to watch your sister?"

"I don't need a babysitter," Sierra pipes from the table, her fingers curled in front of her face so she can blow her nails dry. "Mom'll be home at like ten, right?" She flicks her gaze to me then back to Dad. "So I'll only be alone for an hour or so."

Dad grunts and rubs the stubble on his chin. "And you'll behave? Both of you?"

"Yes," we say together.

His eyes go back and forth between us before he lets out a puff of air. "Okay. But Zoe, you bring your phone and answer it if your sister calls. And Sierra, no friends, and no leaving this house."

We both nod and Dad chugs the rest of his soda. "All right, I'll see you girls tomorrow."

Late shift. Again.

Always really. It bugs me how much he and Mom work, but not tonight. Tonight I need them gone.

The second he leaves I run upstairs to change. I pull out the purple number I was going to wear at the last party and strip down to my undies. The window isn't even open because I'm done with that. I can't do it anymore. I need to forget about those amazing—yes, amazing—few days I had with him. Because it's not... it *can't* be what I really want. I've worked so hard to be *this* person. The girl who goes to parties and gets the boys and who everyone wants to be.

And Zak doesn't want anything to do with that person. Guess I have to live with that.

Plopping onto my bed, I dig my phone from my jeans. There are a few texts and for a second my brain gets real stupid hoping they're from Zak. My stomach does a twist turny thing when I open the messages, then drops when I see they are all from Levi.

I guess I can't blame him for trying to get a hold of me. I never gave him my number—I'm sure one of my friends did—but I did give him some tongue. He's probably waiting for his booty call.

He won't have to wait much longer.

If I'm going to stay popular, and forget Zak, I better do it right this time. Not halfway.

I'll c u @ the party 2nite.

I hit send and toss my phone behind me. There's something stinging behind my eyes, but I shake my head and focus on getting dressed.

Yeah, a party and a new boy will cure whatever is wrong with me.

"You're not going to Hope's, are you?"

Sierra leans against my door frame, not looking at me, but at her feet.

"You going to rat me out?"

"No." She steps in my room and settles on the center of my bed. "*I'm* a good sister."

I roll my eyes and go back to putting on my eyeliner. "You were in the effing hospital. I had to tell Mom."

"I-I know."

My head whips around, and I swipe a big black mark across my cheek. Sierra's not looking at me, she's picking at a loose thread in my comforter. I don't even know how to respond. She's never agreed with me on anything.

She twirls her finger around the thread and yanks it out of my bedspread. "So, you're going to a party?"

I shake my head and grab a wipe to get the eyeliner off my cheek. "I'm not taking you."

"I wasn't asking to go." Her eyes narrow. "I was just curious."

Yeah right. Like I'm going to believe that one. Unless...

"Is someone coming over?"

"What?"

"Is that why you're okay with me leaving? And why you won't tell Mom and Dad? You've got someone coming over, don't you?"

She huffs a huge breath out her nostrils and crawls off my bed. "You know, I'm not as bad as you think I am. I was actually going to bed." Her hair bounces a little as she storms across my room. "Have fun at your party."

And she's gone.

What the heck? That was so not normal Sierra behavior. I think house arrest has done something funky to her brain.

Either that or she's gotten better at lying.

It doesn't matter. I can't worry about what's going through my sister's head when I'm so messed up myself. Split personalities and all.

Time to convince the world, and myself, that I'm happy with the choice I made to redefine myself.

Because I *am* happy with it.

I. Am.

See? There's the smile in the mirror. Now, adjust the boobs... and I'm set.

I don't even look at my bookshelf or my window as I walk out.

"This is the part where you tell me the name of that guy you were gushing about the other day."

Hope gives me a huge grin and runs a stop sign in the process.

Ugh. I wish I could go back to two days ago when that's all I wanted to do… gush. But I *have* to get Zak out of my brain. Shove him so far away I won't remember why the heck I liked him in the first place.

It's not going to work if my friends keep bringing him up.

"No. He doesn't want anything to do with me, so I'm moving on."

"What?!" she squeals, making a jerky stop at a light. "Is he crazy? You're Zoe Livingston!"

I laugh. "I know, right! He doesn't know what he's missing." I'm totally using a joking tone, but I'm half serious. I'm the popular one. Shouldn't *I* be rejecting *him*?

That's usually how the world goes round. But both Zak and I know who the better person is between the two of us.

Oh gosh. *Forget about it, Zoe.*

"Well, I know about twenty guys who are ready to pounce now that you're single. Want to know a few from the list?"

Shaking my head, I force a giggle and flip my hair over my shoulder. "Nah. I just want to have fun tonight."

"That's what I mean." She winks, pulling up against the curb outside Jesse's massive house. "A boy to help you… have fun."

"I got it." 'Cause I do. Levi is target boy number one. After all, he's hecka hot, not a bad kisser—from what I remember of that kiss—he's the perfect person to help me get over the geek next door.

The music pumps through my body before we even get inside. Jesse always has a DJ at his parties because he can afford that type of stuff. This is also why I'm never a party host. People would totally realize I'm a fake with the money stuff. That and it's too much work. Jesse can also hire someone to clean up after. Trust funds. Must be nice.

"Hey bitches!" Keira calls from the table she's dancing on. "It's about time you showed up!"

She hops down and plants a sloppy kiss on my lips then does the same to Hope.

"Holy hell. Someone's had a few shots." Hope laughs as Keira loops her arm through both of ours.

"Come on. Let's dance!"

I wiggle her off. "I'm gonna go find someone," I shout over the music. "I'll catch up with you later."

Hope's mouth pops open, but I don't hear what she says before she's dragged away.

Now to find drummer boy. There's no way I'm going to look in this crowd. I'd be stopped by a million people before I found him. That and Cody is trying to catch my eye. Bleck. He needs to stay the hell away from me tonight or he's going to be punched in his diseased junk. Stupid jackass attacking me then spreading rumors.

Just chalk it up to more things I need to forget.

Someone walks by with a shot and without even thinking, I snag it and toss it back. Whew. That'll help the nerves.

Pulling out my phone, I cross over to a less crowded hallway. After a few hugs and "heys" I send Levi a text.

Where r u?

It's a few minutes before my phone vibrates in my hand, and I have to shake off a guy who appeared out of nowhere to offer me a beer. One shot is usually my limit at these things.

Right here.

Huh? I look up and down the hallway, but I can't see the darn boy anywhere. Taking a step into the next room, a hand wraps around my wrist and whirls me around.

"Hey." Levi smiles as I whack him in the chest. Then I see his eyes rake me over and as he takes in my skin tight dress his face flushes. I pucker my lips as I speak, attaching the strings on Popular Zoe's next victim.

"Hey." Taking his hand, I pull him upstairs. "Let's go somewhere we can talk."

There's not any conversation on the way to the bedrooms, but he's not fighting me. Why would he? Here's the booty call he's been waiting for.

And this will totally make me forget about…

Oh gosh, I can't think about it now. That's why I'm here. To forget.

We get to an empty room—only took two tries to find one without a we're-doing-it-rubber-band on the knob—and I open the door for him.

He walks past me and stands awkwardly in the middle of the

room while I shut the door behind him. "So, what did you want to talk about?"

Pulling him by the arm, I drag him to the bed, shoving him down so I can leap on top of him. He's sitting upright against the headboard as I straddle him. I only see his surprised face for a split second before curling my tongue around his to make my intention clear that I don't want to talk.

I. Want. To. Forget.

He wraps his massive hands around my waist, but instead of pulling me closer, he pushes me back.

"Whoa, Zoe," he says catching his breath. "Hang on a minute."

I ignore him and trace my lips along his jaw line and watch him squirm underneath me. Moving my hands to the button on his pants, I try to pretend I know what I'm doing, that I've done it millions of times.

My hands shake, and Geek Zoe is screaming at me to stop, but I can't. I have to get Zak out of my head. I have to stop fighting between two different versions of myself. I have to take control over this whole thing I've made a mess of.

When I get his zipper down, I take a deep breath and close my eyes before pressing against him through his boxers. My stomach leaps off a cliff. Holy crap. I'm touching a guy's penis. How did I get to this? Do I move my hand around? Or leave it here? Do I keep going downward?

Oh, I'm totally in over my head with this stuff.

"Um, Zoe?" Levi's voice cracks, which makes me feel like maybe I'm doing something right even though I'm just pressing against him.

"Yes?"

"Is everything okay?"

That's a bizarre question, given the position we're in. Crap, I knew I wasn't doing this right. I whip my hand out from his pants and go back to what I know how to do. Making out is just fine anyway. This whole thing is starting to remind me of what Cody did to me and it's making me a bit sick.

"Yeah. I just want you." I flutter my eyes and lean in to suck on his neck. His pulse jumps in my mouth, but he pushes me, gently, so he can look at my face.

"You… you don't seem okay."

I'm totally shaking as I look at him. His eyes are the sexy blue color girls get lost in, and his blond hair could rival Edward Cullen's. And he's staring back at me with concern, honest sincerity. Something I don't want or deserve.

And I feel nothing.

No attraction, no physical pull, no emotional one either. I want to stop thinking. Get lost in someone else so I can erase Zak from my memory. But as I take in his perfection, I wish those blue eyes were darker, his golden bouffant was styled downward covering his eyes, and dyed dark brown.

Damn it.

The heat shoots up my neck. I'm not sure if I'm more embarrassed or angry, and my beast of an attitude screeches through my tone.

"You a virgin or something? Seriously, I'm on top of you. You're not going to take advantage?" Because anyone else would.

"No, Zoe. I'm a virgin, yeah, but that's not why I'm stopping this."

I crawl off him, taking a spot on the floor instead.

"Then why?"

He sits next to me, stroking my hair from my face. It's the sweetest thing ever, but I still don't feel anything. It's not like how I feel when I'm with Zak.

"I'm not one of those guys. I've been trying to get a hold of you these past few days so I could talk to you about what happened."

"It didn't mean anything. That kiss at school. You may not be one of those guys, but I'm one of those girls. You should know that already."

"I don't believe that." His hand moves from my hair to my cheek, stroking it softly with his thumb. "I want to be your friend. If you need someone to talk to."

My forehead crinkles, and I crane my neck so I can see his face. He's joking right? No guy ever wants to be just my friend.

"Why?"

He mashes his lips together, shifting his position so he's closer to me.

"Don't take this the wrong way, but you seem so…" He pauses. Not like the pause people do when they try to search for the right way to say something, but the hesitation before people drop a word they don't *want* to say, but feel like they have to.

"Lost."

I shift away from him, worry lines spreading through my face. He's onto me. Better set him straight. "I'm not lost."

He raises an eyebrow, and my pulse skyrockets. That's Zak's thing. Seems everything about this kid reminds me of *him*. I'm supposed to be forgetting the damn boy! Ugh.

"I'm not," I say again.

"If you weren't lost, you wouldn't have attacked me, twice. You don't even know me."

"That's the point," I say, throwing my head back against the mattress.

"Well, I don't want to be some random guy in your life. The rebound. The one night stand. The guy you use to forget all your problems."

My eyelids snap shut. I won't cry. Not in front of him. "How old are you again?"

He chuckles as he pulls my chin down to look at him. "I'm sixteen, but not naïve. I know what people say about you, but that's not what I like about you."

What people say about me? My popular rep I hope. That I club and hang out with Hope and Keira and I'm someone who can really kiss. That stuff's okay to fly around behind my back. But besides that, I can't imagine anything else but a hot body being the source of anyone's attraction to me. "Then what?"

"Not sure how to put it. Just something in your eyes. Tells me you've got a lot more going on in there." He prods the center of my forehead with his soft fingertips.

"Are you sure you're not older than sixteen?"

Shaking his head and smiling, he tucks a strand of hair behind my ear and says, "Pretty sure. I guess I'm mature for my age. Had to grow up fast, you know? Dad ran off when I was a kid, left my mom, sister and I to fend for ourselves."

There he goes again, reminding me of Zak. It seems like the perfect situation. An acceptable, datable guy who has the qualities of the guy I really want.

But he's *not* the guy I really want.

"I'm sorry."

He shrugs. "Happened a long time ago."

"Still."

"Yeah."

We sit in a tense silence, his eyes flicking over my face, my body, a smile lingering on the corners of his mouth. And every second he's here, makes me ache for someone else.

What was I thinking? Acting like the person people think I am, just because I want to get back at someone for being mad at me. Someone who totally has every right to be pissed.

And I feel dirty. And wrong. This isn't who I am, but who I feel like I *have* to be.

I have to get out of here. Will there be anyone who will help me get over the boy next door?

No. There won't be. Even when I'm Popular Zoe, Zak is all I can think about. Him, and who I am with him.

The room is getting really hot. And stuffy. I get off the floor, tripping a little on my heels. Levi reaches out to help me, and I push him back.

"Don't," I snap.

"Zoe…"

"Please, Levi. Just… just leave me alone."

There's a beer with my name on it.

Chapter 15

Who says drinking helps anything?

The music thumps through my chest as my whole body moves to the beat. I'm dancing with one of the random football players. I think his name is Caleb, but I don't remember. He's got his arms around my front as I slide my butt back and forth against him. I can tell he's totally into me, and my mind is too muddy from alcohol to care about the trouble I can get into.

His lips trace the back of my neck and a goofy grin forms on my face. Then suddenly he's raking his warm tongue across my ear.

Ew.

I shove away from him and head over to the opposite side of the room where they've got all those little shot thingies I tried earlier. I don't know what's in them, but they are super yummy.

"Hey Zoe!"

I blink a few times, looking for whoever is shouting my name. Things are way fuzzy. Like, I'm really trying to remember how I got here.

"Huh?"

"Body shots! Get your hot ass over here!"

That sounds like fun! But I don't know where I am. The room is kind of tilted or something.

I take a step and next thing I know I'm flat on my face.

"Zoe?"

Strong hands clasp my upper arms and pull me up. Bad move, buddy. Stomach turns and I think I'm gonna…

"You okay?"

Yeah, I know he asked me a question. My brain goes on rewind, but my reactions are so slow. I can't think straight with all the stomach sloshing and stuff.

"I gotta find my friends." At least I think this is what I say. It probably came out like, 'I gosha feen ma frindsh'.

I scan the room to find the girls. Someone who looks like Hope is making out with a guy on the plush couches near the DJ. And it looks like Keira's flirting with about three different people by the bathroom. Instead of going to either one of them, I go straight to the kitchen. I want another drink, damn it. I still haven't forgotten what happened with Zak, or what happened with Levi, and I want it banished from my memory.

Alcohol will do the trick if sex won't.

Some kid slaps the shot in front of me. I give him a knowing grin, which probably looks stupid since I'm hammered, and toss the plastic cup back.

"I think that should be your last one," someone says in my ear. I roll my eyes, which is a bad idea because the room shifts, and I end up toppling to the floor.

I hear someone laughing, but a different someone than whoever it is that keeps helping me off my ass.

"Come on, Zoe. I'll take you home."

Levi? I look up and sort of make out his face. Yeah, I think it's him. There are drumsticks hanging out of his back pocket. I feel the earth shift again, and I stumble even though I was just standing there.

"Whoa. Let's get you out of here."

I nod, the slush in my head slopping around. That actually sounds like a good idea. I'm not feeling so hot.

He leads me to his car… I think. And I pass out on the seat.

"Hey." Someone slaps me across the face. "Hey, wake up."

My eyes flutter open. The world is blurry, but I know I didn't take my contacts out last night.

Wait a second. Where am I? Whose car is this?

"Is this your house?"

I rub my face before pressing it against the car window. Yeah, that looks like my house.

"Uh huh."

"Oh good." Levi sighs, and I hear him undo his seatbelt. "I couldn't really understand you when you gave me your address."

Huh. I don't remember that.

"Come on."

Hey, when did he get out of the car? And when did he start carrying me?

Oh gosh, I don't like that. It's making my stomach churn.

"Put me down!"

I push him off, kicking and screaming slurry obscenities.

"Okay, okay." He sets me down, but doesn't leave my side.

No. No. No. My parents *cannot* see him.

"You can go home now."

"I want to make sure you get in okay."

I growl at him before opening my front door a crack. "I'm fine. I don't want my parents to wake up."

Please tell me he understood that through all the slurs.

"All right…" He hesitates, then takes his sweet time getting to his car.

I wait till I see his headlights disappear before opening my door all the way. Everything is still so blurry and spinning and something's not sitting well. It's really hot.

Oh shit.

Bolting off the porch I make it to the bushes in time to spew all over them. Sick. Sick. Sick.

More vomit sprays the ground and I fall to my knees until it passes. Forget drinking. This stuff sucks.

When I stumble back to my feet, I take a few breaths and wipe my chin before going inside. Gosh, I hope Mom is in bed and Dad is still at work. They'll kill me if I'm caught totally smashed. It's dark in the entryway, and everything blurs when I flick on the light and makes my head pound a little. I trudge upstairs and head straight to the bathroom.

Must. Brush. Teeth.

Someone's in the shower. Maybe it's not as late as I thought it was. And it's my shower, so it's probably Sierra. Mom and Dad use their own bathroom. I go in anyway. She's seen me drunk before and I've seen her naked. So nothing new here.

I shuffle through the cabinet, looking for my purple toothbrush, but the one I find is green, and kind of looks like the Hulk is plastered on it. Maybe my drunk eyes want to nerd out right now.

As I brush away all the filth from the upchucked alcohol, a voice echoes through the bathroom.

"Is someone in here?"

My stomach shrinks to the size of a peanut. Zak is in my shower?! What the hell?!

He peeks out from behind the shower curtain and his eyes bug out of his face. "Z-Zoe? What are you doing?" He whips a towel off the rack and climbs out not bothering to shut the shower off.

"What am *I* doing?" I shriek. "What are *you* doing? Get out of my house!"

"Are you drunk?"

I guess *he* didn't understand me through the slurs. But he's got to get out of here! He can't see me like this, and no way will my parents be cool with a naked boy in my shower. I flail my arms, trying to push him out of the bathroom. I kick and yell, making a big fool of myself.

He wraps his hands around my middle, pinning my arms down. "Zoe! You've got to calm down."

I keep yelling, struggling against his wet torso and praying to the Master of Jedi's the towel stays around his bottom half.

I hear him growl, and he whips the shower curtain back open

and tosses me under the water. He turns it to chilling cold and some of my senses jolt back into focus.

Wait. The shower head is on the wrong side. And the shower curtain has glow-in-the-dark Star Trek Enterprises on it.

Oh sweet mother ship.

He leaves me there. Gosh, I hope he's getting dressed. I start shivering and turn the water back to warm.

Holy hell. How did I get here? Someone took me home. Levi? Right after I... wait... Did I have sex tonight?

No. I'm pretty sure Levi stopped me from making that huge-o mistake. Then I drank way too...

Oh my gosh. I almost had sex! With someone I don't even really know. What in the name of World of Warcraft was I thinking?

I feel sick. Not like vomity sick—got rid of that for now—but dirty. And I immediately try to scrub off the filth. I know I'm still dressed. I don't care. I soak my body, dress too, with soap.

Despair crawls all over me, and I fall into my knees. I try to remember how it felt to be happy. Like *really* happy. I mean, I thought I was. I thought being popular and going to parties and hanging out with Hope made me happy. And that stuff does because it keeps me from bawling my eyes out when I hear people are talking about me, but then I think about my books on my shelf. The Comic-Con tickets from a few years ago. The Nintendo games and speaking Elvish and all my awesome T-shirts I wish I could wear in public.

That stuff makes me happy too—even happier when I can share it with someone.

And no matter how hard I try, I can't run away from myself.

A knock comes at the door as I sit in the tub letting the water rinse me off. The soap didn't work. I still feel like crap. And I'm crying which doesn't help my head.

Zak peers in, catching me sobbing like a fool in the tub. He checks over his shoulder and shuts the door behind him before climbing in next to me. Dressed and all.

I tuck into his side and let it all fall out. I'm babbling, telling him how dirty I am, that all I wanted was to forget. To erase everything I've done to him, to me, to everyone. I'm not even sure if I'm making any sense with all the alcohol in my system. It doesn't matter though. He just runs his fingers through my wet hair and doesn't say a word.

Chapter 16

Miracle Hangover drink should taste more like Sunny D.

The water starts to get cold and Zak reaches over to turn on more hot water. I can see a stifled grin when he puts his arm back around me.

"What?" I ask.

"Hmm?"

"What was that look?"

"Just thinking."

I don't prod. I'm also lost in thought. I think I've seen this scene somewhere before. In a movie or something.

His voice rings through the room. "You remember when we saw Casino Royale?"

That's it. My lips turn up in a smile. "Yeah. I was just thinking about that."

My head jostles as he laughs. "I was afraid you wouldn't admit it."

"Admit what?"

"That you remember seeing that movie with me. Pretty sure you wanted to block out all our dorky days."

I swallow hard. "I don't want to block them out."

"Could've fooled me."

I sigh, and try to lighten the conversation. "This isn't *exactly* like James Bond."

"Yeah, the girl wasn't wasted."

"And the guy had just killed about twenty people."

"And you're trying to wash off dirt, not blood."

My forehead crinkles. "Huh?"

"That's what you keep saying. You can't get the dirt off."

"Oh."

He doesn't say anything else. He lets me cuddle into him, and I realize, even in my incoherent state, I really like it here.

My mouth is full of cotton balls. My nose burns with the smell of cologne. My head feels like it's going to fall off... and I kind of hope it does.

What the hell happened last night?

I open my eyes, but things are still dark. My face is stuffed in a pillow. A pillow that smells amazing and it makes my heart grow little wings and flutter around my chest.

Groaning, I push my nose farther into the feathers. I make those embarrassing noises, and I quickly sit up to rid myself of the intoxicating aroma.

Ouch.

"Here," a voice says from the edge of the bed, "take this."

Warm fingers open my hand up and something cold drops in the center of my palm. Wait a second. I'm not taking drugs from a stranger.

I flick my eyes open and they land on Zak's. He's not smiling, but it doesn't look like he's mad either.

Without any argument I pop the pills in my mouth and take the drink from his outstretched hand.

"Bleck." That is so not water. "What the freak is this?"

"Something that'll help the hangover," he says, tipping the glass back up to my lips. "It worked for my mom when…" His face reddens and he shakes his head, making his hair flop. "Just drink it."

My nose scrunches as I take another sip. You'd think I was chugging pig guts on Fear Factor.

"Uh…" Zak scratches the back of his neck, then digs in his pocket. He pulls out my cell. "You should probably call your parents."

How the heck did he get my phone? I reach down the top of my shirt, only half aware that I'm digging around my cleavage for something I know isn't there.

"It fell out when you were… when you tried to…" He stops and shakes his head again, his ears looking like they've spent hours in the sun. "It was in the bathroom, but it didn't get wet."

Tossing the cell on the bed next to me, he gives me a faint smile. "When I get back, that whole thing better be gone." He gestures to the drink in my hand, gives me another sort of grin, then leaves.

Okay.

What. The. Hell?

Last I knew, Zak wasn't even talking to me. And my lame attempt at getting over him resulted in a big fat rejection. Not that I'm too upset about that. Thank the Starships I went after Levi and not Hunter. I'd probably never recover from that stupidity.

What happened after that though? It's so fuzzy.

The pounding in my head won't let me think, and it doesn't help I have to drink this vomit-inducing…

Oh crap. Please tell me I didn't puke on Zak. Is that why I was in the bathroom? And why I'm dressed in one of Zak's Indiana Jones shirts and his… Oh my gosh! I'm in his boxers!

This is way too much for me to handle right now. And I gotta pee. I down the rest of the nasty cure-all and race to the toilet.

There's condensation streaking down the mirror, like Zak kept his door shut after he got out of the shower so all the fog didn't really clear.

Wait. He took a shower while I was here? I guess that's not weird 'cause I was asleep, but just thinking about him naked…

Shit.

"Zo?"

My breathing picks up, and I whip the shower curtain open to see my sopping wet dress hung over a hook and dripping into the tub.

How could I forget I stumbled stupid ass drunk into the wrong house and ended up in a shower with my dream guy?

Oh, that's right. All the alcohol.

Gosh, if I forgot that embarrassing, yet amazing hour in the shower with Zak, what else have I forgotten?

"Zo?" Zak says again.

"Um, be out in a minute!" I call through the door. I have to calm down before I go out there. Splashing water on my face, I mentally yell at myself for thinking alcohol and sex were the answers to my problems. It didn't help me escape at all. It landed me face first back where I was: struggling with two versions of myself. Trying to figure out if hiding Geek Zoe is really worth all this.

But I don't want high school to be like middle school again. I don't know if I can handle it as well as Zak does.

And Zak. Whatever that was last night, it was way more than I deserve. Again he's pulling me back together after I've treated him like shit.

I fill my cheeks and let the air seep out. Sick. My breath is rank! I grab the toothpaste and squeeze some on my finger, scrubbing the inside of my mouth till it's foaming. I can't believe Zak was that close to my face without yacking.

Okay, I'm pretty sure my mouth is as minty as it's going to get. And my head is actually feeling better. There's less pounding and the light isn't stabbing my eyes out.

"Wow," I say as I step back into Zak's room, "that crap drink does work."

"Told you." He sits at his desk and pulls out his Wii controller. "You'll probably be able to go back to sleep now."

Huh? My gaze flicks to his window. It's dark outside. "What time is it?"

The TV snaps on. Mario Party lights up the screen. "About six.

You've only been out a couple hours."

I nod and lay back on the bed, trying not to breathe in his scent. Even my hangover nose thinks it smells yummy.

"Did you call your parents?" he asks, keeping his eyes locked on the video game.

"No."

"You going to?"

Whoa. Something's wrong. He's not looking at me, his voice is all strained like he wishes I was still asleep, or wasn't here, and he selected Donkey Kong on the game.

"Are… are you okay?"

"Fine." He shifts in his seat, resting his elbows on his knees. He's such a liar.

My cheeks puff up and I make my way to him. I don't care if I'm the problem, he's so not okay right now and I don't like seeing him like this.

Parking my butt on the floor next to his chair, I narrow my eyes at him. "You're not 'fine'. What's wrong?"

"What makes you think there's something wrong?"

"You always pick Donkey Kong on Mario Party when something's bugging you."

He cocks his eyebrow and finally looks at me. There's a tiny throb in my head, but I shut my eyes for a second and try to force it back.

"You should go back to bed." His gaze goes back to the game.

No. That's not happening. I move so I'm kneeling in front of him, forcing him to look at nothing but me, but it doesn't work so well. He hits pause and keeps his eyes on the controller.

"I'm not going back to sleep till you tell me what's wrong."

"Why the hell do you care?" His voice is so low, I'm not sure if I caught that right, but I'm pretty sure that's what he said.

And he deserves honesty. After everything he's done for me. After what I did last night.

"I-I want to make you feel better, if I can." Things are totally coming out wrong. All 'cause he makes me so jittery.

His brow furrows and he shakes his head. "Go home, Zo."

If he hadn't just used my nickname, I may have listened, but I don't.

"Please, Zak." Wish he would look at me.

He stands, running a hand across the back of his neck. "You shouldn't be here."

"Why not? Your mom's not home." Or at least, I assume she's not.

"That's not what I mean." He pauses. "We're not… it's not like that between us anymore."

My jaw clenches, and I take my time getting to my feet so I don't let the crappy hangover win over what I have to say to him.

"I'm not leaving."

"Dammit, Zo. I don't want you here. You don't care, and you never did." He opens his bedroom door and waves his hand. "So go home."

I should listen to him. I should head home and forget all about last night. Forget the conversation we had in the car the other day. Forget whooping his butt at Lord of the Rings. Forget when we'd

play video games and trivia all night long. Forget when we kissed…
that one time. It just happened. One night a few weeks after his dad
left, I don't know what I was thinking, or if I was thinking at all. I
wanted to help somehow, make him feel better. Next thing I know
my lips are pressing against his and they didn't leave for a long time.

My first kiss. I'm not sure if it was his. We didn't really talk
about it. But that kiss has never been beat. Even with all the guys
who were more experienced.

I should do what he says and go home. And forget everything.

But I have a reputation of doing things I shouldn't do.

Chapter 17

I'm just as bad as douchebag dad.

I walk to the door and shut it, standing so close to him I can feel his breath on my forehead.

"Sorry, I'm not sure what to do here." I'm about to suck air into my cheeks but I stop myself. "But I hate seeing you like this. And I'm not leaving till I can help fix whatever's wrong."

He finally turns to me, confusion all over his face. Not saying anything, but at least he's looking at me. His dark eyes focus on mine, hair still mussed from the shower and flopping across his forehead. But what gets me most is his lips. Tight in the corners like he's suppressing some giant emotion. Anger, maybe, but it seems more like pain.

He's... oh gosh, he's hurt.

Don't know what comes over me. I don't care that my head is starting to throb again and my whole body aches. This stupid hangover doesn't matter right now. I don't want to see his pain anymore and next thing I know, I'm trying to erase the pain from his lips by pressing them with mine.

He's hesitant at first, refusing to respond and keeping his hands firmly at his sides. Am I still doing things wrong? Or did I just shock the hell out of him? I mean, I don't know how I ended up kissing him, but I don't want to stop. Like, *never* want to stop. So I don't pull away. Instead, I bite on his bottom lip, hoping he'll kiss me back.

And he does. Like, hell yes he does! He gives in with a sexy grunt, picks me up by my butt, and allows me to wrap my legs around his hips.

Ho-lee crap, I like that. A lot.

He whips me around so I'm trapped between him and the door. His tongue slides past my teeth and I suck on it, hoping he'll never take it back. Oh yes, yes, yes. He's the best kisser in the whole freaking world! Even with the frenching, it's not sloppy or gross, it's just so flippin' fantastic!

His fingers linger on my sides as deep moans escape his throat. Damn, that's hot. I can't stop my own passionate noises when his hips press into mine, making the door creak with every movement we make. Oh. My. Gosh. Oh gosh, oh gosh, oh gosh. Everything gets warm as I feel every part of him I've wanted for so long against me. His hand moves from my side to the inner workings of my knee, pulling me closer, which I didn't think was possible.

Is this really happening? Is he letting go of everything I've done to him? Everything I put him through? Does he want me just as much as I want him?

The weird thing is I'm not afraid of this. With every other guy it was so different. Like, it wasn't me kissing them. And when things got too heated I'd jump back in my body and tell them to get their paws off. But with Zak, I'm here... like the real me, Geek Zoe, and she wants this too.

I leave his lips for a moment to kiss behind his ear, biting his lobe and involuntarily moaning as I let him explore my body with his hands. But before I get back to his amazing mouth, he backs off, dropping me flat on my butt.

"No," he says between breaths. "Zoe, I can't." He starts mumbling a whole bunch of sorries and keeps his front from my view.

It takes me a minute to catch my breath and get in a comfortable position on the floor. And for the room to stop spinning. "Why... why not?"

"I can't do it again." He interlocks his fingers behind his head and starts pacing, still keeping his back to me.

"Do what again?"

"This!" He finally turns around. "You. Me. I don't think I have it in me."

"What?" I can feel everything inside my chest tighten. Oh gosh, I don't want to have this conversation. I don't want to hear how horrible I am, because I already know.

"I can't fall for you again, Zo. Especially now."

My eyes widen, but other than that, I try to keep my composure. "Why not?"

"Because I don't know who you are anymore."

There's more tightening in the chest area, and something heavy falls into my stomach as what he says sinks in. "But, you know exactly who I am. You're the *only* one who knows who I am."

"That's my point. Why am I the only one who gets to see both sides of you?"

My eyes drop to the floor. "You should know the answer to that."

"Why should I know? You're so hot and cold. One minute you're the girl who used to be my friend, spouting off inside jokes, playing video games, laughing. But then you become someone who's ashamed of not only me, but yourself." He stops as I take it all in. I don't know what to say because he's right. And I have no idea how to explain it.

"What happened last night?"

I gulp and give him the only answer I have. "I drank. A lot."

"And kissing me just now. Was that some kind of side effect?"

I shrug as waves of stupidity roll over me. "T-that's not why... I-I mean I didn't mean to... It just sort of happened."

"Like before? It just happened and then you..."

He pauses for a second, and I shift on the floor to my knees in case I need to bolt from the room crying.

"Look," he says, his voice softening, "my dad left when I was thirteen. My mom was a mess, and she used work to help her escape it all. I only had one thing." He pulls me up from the floor. "You."

My heart thumps an extra beat as his eyes meet mine, and he drops my hand.

"You took my mind off everything. Playing video games, going to conventions, watching Lord of the Rings all in one day and repeating the Elvish language to me. You made me laugh, and it was something I could only share with you."

"Is that why it's important to you?" I whisper.

He ignores me. "I couldn't help but feel something more for you. I thought you felt it to, but then things got all screwed up."

I wrap my arms around myself, trying to hide the word "guilt" which I'm sure is painted all over my body. He turns away, and leans his forehead against his door before punching the wood with his fist.

"You cut me out, Zo. The one person who helped me through everything, and you left. Just like he did."

My mouth drops. Is that seriously how he feels? Comparing me to his prick of a dad?

Crap, he's totally right though. I did bail. I didn't think it was possible to sink into a lower spot than I was before, but here I am, plummeting down into the pits of emotional hell.

"And now both of you are trying to get back in my life, without so much as an 'I'm sorry'."

He turns back around, his hair falling in his eyes. They're watery, but he's not crying. It's more like he's torn. So frustrated with himself. His dad. Me.

"I never left," I mutter. "Not really." Because Geek Zoe is still here.

The corner of his mouth twitches. "Yeah, with you, it seems worse. I have to see you every day. I see you fall short of who you could be all the time. I hear things about you. Things I know can't be true because you're better than that. And hating myself for thinking, what if you're not? What if everything is true? And you've become a different person? And I've lost you forever?"

"You'll never lose me." He won't. I'm still me… somewhere,

and especially with him. I'm still *me*.

He shakes his head and doesn't look at me. I cross the room and grab his face, forcing those dark eyes to look into mine.

"I'm. So. Sorry. For everything." Crap here come the water works. I sniffle and try to push them away. "I still feel everything for you. Still…" I want to say it but I can't. Not now. Not after being compared to his dad. Not after everything I've put him through over the past few years. Saying everything I feel for him would be wrong right now. "Care for you."

His eyes tighten, and I hope he's ready to give into me again. But his voice comes out low and hurt, tossing my expectations for anything more with him right out the window.

"I don't believe you."

I've lost the ability to breathe. Like I've been shot with poison directly in my lungs. "What?"

"I don't believe you're sorry."

Now my breathing is abnormal, like hyperventilating to the point of passing out. "Why not?"

"What'll happen on Monday, Zo? When we're back in school and I want to hold your hand in the hallway? When I want to say more than two words to you? When I want you to sit with me at lunch?"

I don't answer. I can't answer without it hurting either one of us.

"Yeah, that's what I thought." He wiggles from my hold, and I let him, still too stunned and hurt and guilty to move at all.

I hate crying. It seems like it's all I ever do. And I will *not* cry in front of him again. He's not the reason why I feel like this.

I am.

"Um, can you forget about this?" I wish I didn't have to ask that so much. And really wish my voice didn't crack a million times in that sentence.

His dark eyes shine as he looks at me, his face fighting between hurt and concern. He still worries about me, even after all I've done. I so don't deserve him.

He finally opens his mouth to say something, and I can tell he's still fighting his torn emotions. "I don't want to forget. Even though you were backwards drunk," He reddens as his eyes flick to his bathroom, "you're close to the girl I used to know."

I try to smile, but not sure how it looks. Maybe I can get in some sort of, I don't know, gratitude or something, because I totally sucked at that. And because he needs to know I *do* care about him. "Um, thanks for helping me last night. My parents would've killed me if I… yeah. So, thanks."

He nods, shuffling his feet. He grabs his jacket and walks over to me.

"Come on, I'll make sure you get home okay."

Chapter 18

I think my mind is becoming bi-polar.

It's freezing outside, and Zak offers his jacket to me, even though we're only walking like ten feet.

"Thanks."

He nods, squeezing his hands into his front pockets. I stop at my door, turning around to look at him at the bottom of my porch.

This is so crazy. My mind is trying to hit the rewind button to let me know how the heck I ended up here. Not at my porch, but like, in this situation. My used-to-be best friend not wanting anything to do with me. And me still wanting everything with him. Even after all the drinking and trying to forget the hole I've put myself in, I still... I still want him.

Even more, I want what I had with him.

He turns to leave, and I blurt the only thing running through my aching head.

"Let me make it up to you."

He stops, tripping a little as his mouth hangs open. "W-what was that?"

My eyes go straight to my feet and I do a blowfish imitation. "I want to make it up to you. I want to try, I mean do you think it's possible for us to be friends again?" Gosh, please say yes.

He cocks his eyebrow and my stomach trips over itself. "Honestly? I don't know."

I take a deep breath, making sure it doesn't stay in my cheeks. "What if I could prove to you I can be your friend?"

His mouth turns upward into that unbelievably sexy smirk. "How?"

How? *How?* Hmm…

Oh!

"Will you take me for another driving lesson?"

He hesitates, giving me the are-you-serious? expression.

"I promise I won't hit your seat release. And maybe we could go out to dinner or something."

"Like in public?" His smile comes back, and I have to remember what the crap I was saying.

"Yeah." My voice falters, shaking so bad with the decision I'm making. What he said this morning… all of it, makes sense. I can't be ashamed of him anymore. Or myself. I know it's easier said than done, but I'm going to try to get Geek Zoe to win the battle over insecurity.

He goes up the steps to stand on the porch, coming so close his breath tickles my nose as he searches my eyes. He won't find anything. I'm being sincere.

"Okay," he says taking a step back. "What time?"

As soon as possible. I don't know how much longer I can wait to be with him again. "Uh, five?" I wish I would've offered lunch instead, but I think I need to sleep off the rest of this hangover.

"Today?"

"Yeah."

"Are you sure you're up for that? I mean, even with that stuff I gave you, you're probably dealing with a huge headache."

Yes, but I don't care. "I'll sleep it off."

For whatever reason, this makes his ears go bright red, and he wipes his hands on his jeans.

"S-sounds good, I guess. I'll come by at five, but if you're still feeling like junk, we're not going anywhere." He leaps off the steps, smiling at his perfect landing before he turns back to me. "Oh, and Zo?"

"Yeah?"

"I really hope you're being serious. I don't think I have much forgiveness left."

I nod, hoping my enthusiasm will show I'm not going to disappoint him. 'Cause I won't.

I won't.

Right?

He smirks. "See ya tonight, then."

A goofy smile takes shape on my face as I watch him walk away, happy he didn't ask for his jacket back. I curl into it, breathing in his smell and trying to forget how awful a person I am to him. When I get to my room, I talk to myself in the mirror.

"All right. Listen up," I say pointing a disciplining finger at my reflection. "You've got one shot to fix this. Don't. Screw. It. Up. You've hurt him too much. You *can't* do it again."

Suddenly, my worried and neurotic behavior rears its ugly head. *What if someone sees us?*

"It doesn't matter," I answer myself in the mirror.

What if they spread rumors I'm into all that geeky stuff?

"It would be true. It's nothing to be ashamed of."

But it is! No one would look at me the same.

"Do you like the way they look at you now?"

They envy me! Girls want to be me and guys want to be with me. I'm talked about because I'm popular and they're jealous, not because I'm an easy bully target. That's what I want.

"But do you want to be you, the real *you*, more?"

I whisper the last question to myself, glancing from the mirror to Zak's bedroom window. He seems to know who I am, but do I even know who I am anymore?

My eyes flick to my bookshelf.

Yeah, *that's* who I am.

I take in another breath of his jacket, the early morning swirling around me. The way his hands felt against my skin. The sweet taste of his tongue gliding with mine. The heat in my pelvis as he pressed himself against it. It was better than before, when all we did was kiss a few times. This was something much deeper. Like he's been struggling with the same urges I have, but been keeping himself at a distance because of what he said. He doesn't really know me anymore.

That's another thing I can't stop thinking about. Even when he jumped away, and told me to stop, he bore his soul to me. Opened up in a way no one else has. Told me exactly how he feels, and how I can fix it.

And I'm *going* to fix it.

Without removing his jacket—or anything else of his I'm wearing—I slide between my sheets, still feeling all in a flurry from the entire night. It totally didn't happen the way I thought. But instead of feeling guilty and sad, which I should totally feel considering the whole drunken stupor, I feel anxious—excited I have the chance to make it up to him.

Closing my eyes and grinning, I let my mind go to romantic places. At least, romantic for me and Zak. Hogwarts, Middle Earth, Voyager, and I laugh as I think about the Millennium Falcon, since we'll be in my car later. I still can't believe all these things remind him of what I was to him. That it wasn't an obsession, but something that helped him through a difficult situation. I guess that makes me the real dork, since I don't have any deeper meaning for the geeky stuff. Just that it's pretty much awesome.

I sigh, stretching out and cuddling into his jacket. My mind won't shut off though, and my body feels like it's been chopped up in an engine turbine and mashed back together. After an hour of fumbling around under the sheets, I give up on sleep and get one of the books from my nerdy collection.

The *Guide to World of Warcraft* catches my eye. I think the last time I flipped through its pages was a few years ago. Leaping back on my bed, I get ready to toss my comforter over me, but I pause.

I'm not hiding anymore. This can be good practice for me.

Taking a deep breath, I open the book before I lose my nerve.

The pages look brand-new. The picture of the Death Knight

almost looks real. I trace the patterns on the thick armor and scary complexion. It looks total badass, and I get the urge to play the game, ready to annihilate any and all competition.

I flip the page to the blood elves. Holy hell! What is that? There's a handwritten scribble in the margin! I would *never* write in one of my books, especially the WoW one. Putting the book closer to the light, I squint to make out what it says.

Thanks for everything Zo! Better study up for our tournament this weekend. I'm gonna wipe the floor with you! —Zak

My elated feelings get swept away as I read his words, guilt replacing them instantly. As my eyes fill to the brim, I slam the cover of the book and chuck it across the bed.

I'm so naïve to think I can change everything overnight. That tournament was the first time I ditched him. I went to a party instead because they actually invited me. I ended up wasted and making out with another guy. Someone who's way popular and crowd pleasing. Totally brought me into Popular Zoe's realm. I technically didn't cheat on Zak, since we were never really together, but I'm sure it felt that way to him.

Crapola, not much has changed since then, has it?

And you know what sucks? I didn't even care. I was too happy to finally feel accepted I didn't even apologize. I didn't say a word to him about it. I kept my window shut and curtains closed and went out and partied every chance I could. Next time I saw him was in school. He was even nice to me then, and I shoved him aside like he meant nothing to me. All because he reminded me of the stuff I was made fun of for.

Holy crap! Why is he willing to give me another chance? After everything I've put him through. Here I am feeling all mushy gushy over his kisses when they never should've happened. I don't want to be that girl—the girl who uses sex and alcohol to solve everything. The girl I was last night. Zak doesn't want that girl either. How the heck did I think kissing him was a good idea? I'm the most selfish person in the world.

I glance at the clock, trying to focus my eyes through the watery blur. It's almost eight-thirty, and definitely not the time to call and cancel since he's probably crashed out from being up all night too. Maybe I can pretend to be sick or something. I mean, I do feel pretty effing awful. But would that be better or worse than going out with him? I don't want to mess this up, but now the building pressure of it all makes me feel like I don't stand a chance of fixing anything.

I grab the back of my head and pull it to my knees as I struggle with all my guilt, bawling until there's no liquid left in me. Somewhere between confidence and insecurity, I finally drift off to escape my jumbled mind.

Chapter 19

Good thing my bath mat is clean.

"Where are we going?"

"You'll see in a minute."

Zak has one hand over my eyes and the other clasped in my fingers as he stands behind me, whispering in my ear. It feels so good to have him this close, I can't help but giggle and grin like one of those Twi-hards whenever they see a poster of Taylor Lautner.

He moves me forward, pressing against my back and keeping his face tucked by my shoulder. At this point, I don't care where the heck we're going. I kind of hope we never get there.

"Okay," he whispers, and goose bumps crawl everywhere his breath hits, "you ready?"

I nod so fast he laughs at my enthusiasm. Then he drops his hand from my eyes.

Major nerdgasms. I'm standing in the middle of what looks like a movie set. There's no one around. Dead quiet, but I know exactly what movie set he brought me to.

"Transformers?"

"What do you think?"

"I thought they would've torn it down already. The movie's been out for a few years."

Zak smiles and turns me so I can look at him. "I called in some favors."

"Wow. You did all this since this morning?"

He nods and tucks his hand into mine. "Of course. I knew you'd like it."

Holy hell I like it! This is frakking amazing! I lean up to kiss him, because I just have to, but before I get there, someone calls out from behind me.

"Hey!" Keira pops out from behind the huge replica of Bumblebee waving to someone behind her. "They're over here! I *told* you she wanted to deflower Dork Lord."

Crap. It's not just Keira. It's everyone. Even teachers. Everyone at my school swarms behind her, throwing out awful names and laughing at us.

Zak doesn't even do anything. He's still smiling at me, waiting for me to kiss him, or respond somehow. Like he's totally oblivious to the girls making fun of his lack of abs, and his plaid overshirts and Star Wars keychain. I mean all the stuff they say about him pisses me off because Zak is so much better than what they see, but what they say about me hurts so much I can't find the strength to defend him.

I try to block it all out, slamming my hands over my ears and closing my eyes. But it still hits me. Like the volume turns up when I do and their faces are more focused.

My chest is so tight, and my stomach churns as I shrink to the floor. I want it to stop. Everything. What they're saying and how it affects me.

Zak leans down and cups my face.

"Zoe?"

I don't answer him. I can't.

"Zoe!"

I open my eyes, but things blur, and he releases his hold on me. He smirks and then starts tapping on my face.

What the crap?

"Zoe!"

My eyes pop open, and I shoot upright. My hair is matted in sweat, and Zak's jacket hangs loose off my shoulders exposing Indiana in all his mighty glory across my chest. I hear a chuckle from the side of the bed.

"I know I'm early, but I can't believe you're still asleep."

I rub my eyes and shake my head, making sure I'm actually awake this time. "Sorry, I didn't sleep well."

"Yeah. You looked like you were having weird dreams." His eyebrows pull together. "You okay? Do we need to do this another time?"

No. I'm not really okay. But how can I tell him what I'm so worried about without screwing up this chance I have to make things good between us? Yeah, I can't. So I lie.

"I'm totally fine. Just waking up." I attempt a smile. "How did you get in here?" Even if my parents were home, there's no way they'd let a boy go to my room.

That perfect smile stares at me as he stands. "You're not the only one who can jump the distance between our windows. When you didn't answer your front door, I got worried."

"That I was ditching you?" I accuse, narrowing my eyes and pulling the sheets tight around me.

"No silly girl. I worried maybe something happened. You didn't answer your cell either."

I glance at my nightstand where my phone is plugged in. Guess I forgot to take it off silent.

"Sorry, I didn't think to set my alarm." It still amazes me his first reaction is always worry. Is it wrong to think someone can be so perfect for me? But of course, I'm not perfect for him so it doesn't really matter.

"Did you still want to go?" he asks, his face falling a little. "Or is last night's party still giving you headaches?"

No. There's a bit of a throbbing between my eyebrows, but it's nothing a few Advil won't cure. And I'm not sure if I want to *go* anywhere. I want to stay here and hide out with him, if I'm being honest. I can't do that though if I'm going to prove to him I want to be his friend again.

Crap. I'm so gonna mess up tonight.

"Yes, I still want to go. But can I take a shower first?" I still feel all party dirty and I need some heat to loosen the knots in my chest.

He nods, the sexy grin that sets my heart on fire planted on his face. I smile in return, allowing myself to enjoy this moment *before* I turn into insecure mulch.

"I'll be quick," I promise. "You can wait here."

He raises his eyebrows, but plops down on the bed next to me, stretching across the pillows. He doesn't look comfortable though, and he shoves his hand under his back and pulls out the WoW book.

"Ah!" he exclaims, waving it by his face. "This book is wicked awesome."

I laugh, punching him in the shoulder. "Good, at least you'll be entertained."

As he flips open the pages, I suddenly have the urge to kiss him again. To knock the book out of his hands and replace them with me.

I hold the breath in my cheeks and try to calm down. *Get a freakin' hold of yourself Zoe!*

Tucking his jacket around my body, I skip to the bathroom as quickly as I can. I know I have no right to think it, but I kind of hope he checked my ass out as I left.

I give myself another pep talk as I scrub off all the sweat from my dream. Zak seems like he's in a good mood, and so far I haven't managed to screw anything up. But the real test will be out there. In front of people. Possibly running into kids from school, or their parents or siblings.

My stomach twists, like it's wringing itself out, trying to get rid of all the excess emotions in my body. Leaving only nerves.

These kind of nerves I can handle. The ones right before you go out with a guy you really want to go out with. Better these nerves than those stupid ones about being spotted doing something embarrassing.

Zoe! It's not embarrassing! Stop thinking like that!

The water shuts off with a squeal. The steam that fills the room makes it hard to see as I fling the curtain open and reach for the towel rack.

But my hand only grabs air.

You've got to be kidding me!

And of course, the only way to get to a towel is through my room. If this was any other guy, coming out naked would be fine, expected even. But Zak doesn't want that girl. He wants the real me. And the real me wishes I was invisible right now.

Panic mingles in with my nerves as I search for an alternative. My eyes land on the toilet paper, which won't work and makes me shake my head laughing. *Don't be ridiculous, Zoe.* There's nothing under the sink. I consider taking the shower curtain down, but then the bath mat catches my attention.

That should work.

Wrapping it around my body, rubber side out, the cushy side clings to my wet skin and I send praises that I washed the dang thing the other day.

I look ridiculous, but at least I'm not walking out stark naked.

"Uh, Zak?" I say through the door

"Mmm?" His tone tells me he's totally absorbed in the book. Good.

"Can you not look? I forgot to grab my clothes."

I hear him laugh. "I've seen you in less than a towel, but yeah. I won't look if you don't want."

"Well, I forgot a towel too."

I'd pay to see his face. The silence makes me wonder what he's thinking, and I open the door a crack to get a glance of it.

He's not there. He's disappeared. Like he's some sort of superhero, like The Flash, which would be awesome.

"Zak?"

"I-I'm in the hall. Just let me know when you're dressed."

I drop the bath mat on the floor, relieved I don't have to come out in it. Though funny, it would be mortifying.

The towels I haven't folded yet are at the bottom of my hamper, so I have to dig around to get one, drying off on the other clean clothes in the process. When I finally find two, I wrap one on top of my head and quickly pat down the rest of my body with the other.

I toss the towel on the bed, grabbing a bra and panties. My hands shake so bad I can't put my underwear on without falling on my face. I plummet to the floor with a loud thud.

"Are you okay in there?" Zak asks, laughing.

"Yeah! I'll be done in a minute, sorry."

Why can't I find anything to wear? All the short and slutty crap doesn't seem to fit the situation, and all the dorky shirts are a little too much for me right now. Why do I not own anything in between?

I settle on a pair of jeans and a low cut yellow top, wearing a cami underneath it, though I normally wouldn't have. But Zak isn't impressed by cleavage or how much skin I show.

I braid my hair quickly, and skip makeup, being all too aware he's waiting for me.

Taking a deep breath, I open the door and Zak falls back in between my legs. I burst out laughing.

"Sorry," I say through my giggles.

He rubs his head, chuckling along with me. "Ow."

"Get up." I kick him. "I'm starving."

His whole face brightens with my enthusiasm to get going. Maybe this will be easier than I thought.

"Okay," he says, hopping to his feet. "Where do you want to go?"

My voice gets stuck in my throat as I try to think of places we'd be less likely to run into people. *Damn it, Zoe! Stop with the insecure bullshit.*

Maybe this won't be easy.

He saves me from answering, gauging my eyes. "How about we wing it?"

I nod and imitate a chipmunk storing nuts for the winter. He smiles and squeezes my cheeks together, then lets his fingers trace down my neck, my shoulder, my arm, landing in my hand.

"Okay, let's go." I tuck into his arm and shout to myself. *Do not mess this up!*

Chapter 20

Let the battle of the Zoes begin!

I start the car all by myself. Like a big girl. But I kind of wish he would've helped.

"What is this?" he says, making a face at the radio.

"Jason Derulo," I sing as Jason sings it. Zak laughs and promptly turns off the music.

"Not a fan?"

"Ugh, no."

I raise an eyebrow, but I'm sure it doesn't look as awesome as when he does it, and he stumbles over his words.

"I mean, *you* have a good voice. I-I just meant mainstream totally sucks. N-not to bash on your taste in music, but… what is so funny?"

My hand claps over my mouth, stifling all my giggles. "I'm sorry," I say bringing my hand down. "It's like you're trying to dig yourself out of a hole, when I didn't feel offended in the first place."

He pokes my side, tickling me. "Get the car to the street, silly girl."

I love it when he calls me that. Mental note: be dorky. "Will you help me?"

"I thought you did pretty well without it last time."

I know I'm pushing my luck, but I don't care. So far I haven't done anything wrong. I'm going to take advantage of it. Grabbing his hand with my left, I force it on top of my right hand on the shifter.

"Please?" I say as I tuck his fingers in between mine. His face flushes and I see his Adam's apple move up and down as he gulps. I can't help the strings tugging my lips, and he smirks at my goofy grin.

"All right," he says in defeat. "But you *will* have to learn to do it all by yourself."

I roll my eyes, and he moves my hand into reverse.

Instead of being nervous, Zak actually has a calming effect on me. I don't stall the car once. Score!

"Wow, have you been practicing?" he asks after I get going on a hill without plowing into the person behind me.

I roll my eyes and pretend like his compliment totally didn't just make my freaking day. "Hey, do you mind if we stop somewhere?"

"Whatever you want. You're driving."

Stopping the air that wants to fill my cheeks, I pull into the Walgreens parking lot and shut the car off.

His eyebrow shoots up, but he doesn't say anything. Just fumbles around with his seatbelt before bolting around the car to open my door for me.

Cute.

Now let's not screw this up.

I so want to hold his hand, so I keep it nonchalantly at my side waiting for him to "accidentally" bump into me.

No such luck.

"What are we here for?" he asks, shrugging his hands into his pockets, his light saber keychain lighting up as he hits it.

I tug him by the overshirt to the oral hygiene section. Running my finger through all the different selections, I finally land on a toothbrush and wave it by my face. "Is green still your favorite color?"

He chuckles. "You're buying me a toothbrush?"

"I thought you needed a new one. You know, 'cause I got yours all nasty."

That darn sexy smile creeps on his lips. The one I don't ever deserve and yet he still gives me. "I'm surprised you even remembered using it. I thought you were too wasted to remember anything from last night."

I shove the toothbrush against his chest and nearly pass out because I touched him.

"Well, going into the wrong house and walking in on you in the shower has been burned into my brain." Holy crap! Did I really just say that? I know I'm flaming red now. How do I take it back without making it worse?

He raises his eyebrows, his eyes totally laughing at me. I wish my legs didn't feel like Jell-O, because I kind of want to get out of here.

So much for trying to be nice. This was such a bad idea. Mentally smacking myself in the forehead.

"I guess that would traumatize you." Now his face has reddened.

"I didn't see anything," I say quickly. Could this conversation get any more uncomfortable? "I was just saying because, you know I was drunk and you were—"

"Naked." He's laughing now.

Yes. The conversation could get more uncomfortable.

"How would you feel if you walked in on *me* naked?" What is wrong with my mouth today?

"Hmm…" He rubs his chin and attempts pervert eyes. It looks so funny I can't help but burst out laughing.

"Shut up!" I smack his shoulder and he steps back. As if I could really rock him off his feet with that weak hit.

"Well, thanks," he says, handing the toothbrush back, "and yeah, green is still my favorite color."

"Good." I walk past him, covering my heated face. I can't believe I talked about his naked ass. Totally not what I had in mind for this… whatever this is.

"So, where did you want to eat?" I ask when we get back in the car and reverse out of the parking lot.

"You're driving."

Is that going to be his cop-out for making any decisions today?

"Well, do you want to go in somewhere? Or just grab something to eat in the car?"

"Up to you."

Argh. I feel like this is one of those scenes with the bomb wires. And if I cut the wrong one, that'll be it for my chances with dream nerdboy.

I know I should prove to him I'm okay with us being seen

together—which I'm still not one-hundred percent sure I am okay with, and that sucks—but I really want to be alone with him. Great. Just *lovely!* Here I go with the battle of the Zoe's.

"You okay?" he asks.

I nod. "Just hungry. Trying to decide what I want."

"Be honest," he says, putting his hand on mine and shifting into third.

Forcing back laughter at my transparency, I blow out my cheeks as I consider granting his request.

"Zo," he prods.

"I don't want to tell you." That's honest.

"Why not?" He shifts as we come to a stoplight, fully smiling now.

"Because you might get mad."

As soon as the words leave my mouth, his smile disappears. "You don't want to be seen with me."

"No, no!" I blurt. Gosh, I don't want him to think that even if it's a tiny bit true. And I hate myself for admitting to that, but my freaky dream keeps coming back and haunting me. "That's not what I meant. I don't mind going someplace public like I promised, but it's just…" There goes my voice evaporating like it always does when I get scared.

"The light's green."

I let off the clutch, jerking a little, but not stalling. "Sorry."

"What were you saying?"

The engine revs really loud and he moves his hand from mine to my leg and pushes it down on the clutch. Then he quickly shifts with his other hand. The car quiets as the rpm's drop.

"Wow, you're good." I smile trying not to drool over how hot that was.

"Pay attention, Zo." He chuckles and I get my courage back.

"I want to be alone with you."

He's still leaning toward me, his eyes flick up to my face, and I totally want to meet his gaze, but I don't want to crash the car.

"Why?"

"Because."

A small puff of air hits my neck as he huffs. "Because why?"

"I'm not trying to avoid people. It's just, I-I…" I let out a defeated sigh when I can't explain without telling him exactly what I want, which is a chance for Geek Zoe to be herself without worrying over everything else. He totally helps me do that, when we're…

"You just want to spend some time alone?"

Exactly. "Yes."

He pauses and my face gets hot.

"Uh, yeah. That sounds okay."

My stomach does a little ribbon dance as he agrees. "Okay, then you choose the food."

His wide smile distracts my gaze for a second, and I have to snap it back to the road.

"Panda."

Chapter 21

Always bring a compact when you go out to eat.

"Mmm." Damn those uncontrollable moans, but the mandarin chicken from Panda is made by gods.

Zak leans back against the windshield of my car, rubbing his flat stomach and gazing at the surrounding trees. "I think I might explode."

Even after stuffing himself silly, he's so damn sexy. I smile and move the chicken into my cheek so I can talk. "Well, if you didn't eat so fast, you probably wouldn't have eaten so much. Did you even save me any Chow Mien?"

He pinches his fingers leaving a tiny bit of space between them. I laugh and continue chewing my food, letting the cool mountain air brush over my face. It's lucky we live so close to spots like this, where we can escape the city and park on the side of the road, listening to the rapid water kissing rocks in the stream—smelling the pine and maple trees, and tasting the fruit filled air.

Totally like Lord of the Rings. Which is perfect for us.

After I finish my chicken and the two bites of Chow Mien he

left me, I grab the bag with the fortune cookies in it. Hey!

"Did you eat yours already, cheater? You know it doesn't come true until everyone has finished eating."

"No." He leans up on his elbows. "Did they only give us one?"

"Looks like it." I pull it out and hand it to him. "You can have it."

Smiling, he takes it from my hand, which surprises me. I expected us to argue over the stupid thing.

"This is perfect. Now it can be like a wishbone." He bites off the wrapper and sticks one side of the cookie out to me.

"Cheesy," I tease in a sing-song voice, but I take the other side and pull. It splits down the middle and the paper lodges in his half.

"That's what you get for making fun of me." Zak winks, sticking his piece of cookie in his mouth and pulling out the fortune.

I play with my own half, fingering the edges. We used to do this. All. The. Time. Split our cookies open and add silly crap on the end, always something to do with Harry Potter. Gosh, how could I have given up something so awesome? I totally ruined our friendship.

"Geez, I didn't know you'd be so torn up about it." He chuckles as he sticks the paper in between his fingers and holds it out to me.

Guess I'm transparent today.

"I don't want the stupid fortune." I shove his hand away, smirking. "I was just thinking."

"About?"

"You." Ugh. Here comes the word vomit.

"What about me?" He slides closer, pulling me down next to him on the windshield. His hands shake a little on my arm. "That

I'm so incredibly sexy eating my cookie?" He sticks his tongue out so he can show me his "see food."

"You caught me," I say, shoving him. We laugh, our bodies moving in tune with each other. That totally gives me the good kind of chills.

When our amusement subsides, he wraps his arm around me. "Really, Zo. What were you thinking about?"

"What a crap friend I've been."

I think I've pulled him up short. He doesn't speak, but it looks like he wants to. I drop my eyes, knowing he can't say anything reassuring without lying to me.

Clearing my throat of all the gook that suddenly appears there I say, "I'm sorry. I know you don't believe me, but I *am* sorry for hurting you."

He coughs and I glance at him from under my eyelashes. His head's turned the other way.

"I'm starting to," he says.

"Starting to what?"

He looks at me. "Believe you."

I think I may pass out. His face moves closer and my heart pumps in my head. He reaches his other arm across my body, and tucks the fortune in my hand.

"You can have it," he says softly, pressing his forehead against mine. "Friends like to share." He smiles and it sends a torrent of electric shocks through my chest.

"We're friends again?"

"Baby steps."

It's like I don't have control over my body because kissing him is definitely not "baby steps" and that's exactly what I try to do. Apparently I have no self control.

My lips barely brush his before he pulls back, taking his sexy scent with him.

"Sorry," I mumble, slapping my forehead. "I wasn't thinking."

He laughs and tucks me into his side. "It's not that, Zo."

"Then what?"

He pulls out a napkin and hands it to me. My heart falls from my head to my butt as he holds in his laughter.

"Are you kidding? I've had crap on my face this whole time and you haven't said anything?"

He rolls over, barking out his amusement as I scrub my lips, my cheeks, even my eyebrows. I chuck my napkin at him and push him so hard he almost falls off the hood of my car.

"Whoa crap!"

I nudge him farther, giggling nonstop as I try to push him off. He puts his hands up in defense, but I clasp onto them, moving my legs on either side of his hips and pinning him down. We're both laughing so hard, tears stream down my face, and he can't seem to breathe.

And I love every frakking second of it. How long has it been since I've laughed like this?

Falling onto him, I move my hand to the empty Chinese box, wiping a finger across the side. I've got him now, 'cause he totally doesn't notice. His expression actually gets really serious. His eyes search mine, then my lips, then my hair as he reaches up with a shaking hand to play with the strands that have fallen in my face.

I almost let him kiss me, but the urge to get him back wins out and as he leans in, I wipe mandarin sauce across his nose. Laughing like a mad woman, I roll off him, landing awkwardly on the ground and try to lock myself safely in the car.

He catches my hips before I can get to the handle, spins me around and traps me against the door. I scream as he wiggles his nose all over my face.

"Stop! Stop! You win!" I say through yells and giggles. He's laughing with me and I can't believe how incredibly dorky we are… and how cute he looks even with sauce all over his face.

"Success." He smiles and we stare at each other as we catch our breath. But my breathing only gets quicker, my heart rate going as fast as the tempo in the chicken dance song after it plays for a while.

"Zak?"

His eyes sparkle when I say his name. "Hmm?"

I don't care we're both a mess right now. All that swims through my brain is how happy he makes me. And how much I want him. *This* guy.

"Can friends kiss?"

He drops his smile. Crap. I can see the argument he has with himself behind his eyes now that I'm giving him the chance to think about it.

He pulls away, not answering me and grabs the rest of the napkins. Handing me a few and wiping his own face, he says, "You ready to get going?"

I nod, staring at the napkins in my hands. My limbs seem to

have forgotten how to move. I should've let him kiss me instead of getting even. Darn competitive nature.

"It's not that I don't want to, Zo." He takes the napkin from my palm and wipes my face for me. "I don't think we can be friends that kiss. Didn't work out so well last time."

I nod again. He's totally right. And I don't want to be just his friend, but I don't know how I'll handle him as a boyfriend without disappointing him.

"Well, let's go. Do you mind driving?" I ask as I gather up the trash on the hood and chuck it in a garbage can chained to a tree.

"No, you need practice."

I grimace at him. "Fine. But you still have to shift for me."

"You just want to hold my hand," he says pointing a finger and smirking.

"Well, duh."

I can't believe this surprises him after I asked if he would kiss me. But his eyebrows disappear into his bangs and his mouth drops as he struggles to respond. Cute.

"Oh, well. Okay." He blushes. "But you have to be the one to shift."

"Deal."

I go to open my door, and he yells like I'm about to run over a cat. "Wait!" He jogs to my side and lifts the handle, but the door doesn't open. He tugs on it with both hands, wiggling it up and down like it'll suddenly start working.

Laughing, I ask, "You having a bit of trouble there?"

He cocks his head, exaggerating the roll of his eyes. "Keys?"

I press my hand against my pocket. My flat pocket. My eyes pop and I peer into the car window and sure enough, they're dangling from the ignition.

"Whoops."

Chapter 22

I must be PMS-ing with all the mood swings.

Zak laughs and whips out his cell.

"What are you doing?"

"Calling Ariana."

It's like a fire-breathing dragon hatches in the pit of my stomach. "Why?"

"Calm down. She's got my truck. She can pick us up and you can get the spare key from your house." He pauses to look at me. "You do have a spare, right?"

"Yes," I snap, folding my arms and leaning against my car. Why the hell does *Ariana* have *Zak's* car? "We aren't going to leave my car here though with the keys inside are we?"

He shakes his head and presses the phone to his ear. I try not to unleash the ravenous beast growing inside me as he talks to her.

"She'll be here in a few minutes." He shoves his phone back in his pocket.

"Great." I knew I'd ruin the date by doing something stupid. Now I have to share Zak with Clingy Girl.

"Hey," he says as shuffling his feet in the gravel. "She's my friend."

"Like me?" I raise a questioning eyebrow which I'm sure gets lost in translation, since I can't do it right.

His hair flops around as he shakes his head at the dirt. "No one will ever be like you."

Freaking Spiderman, I'm going to maul him if he keeps saying cheesy crap like that.

Sliding down the car door, I plant myself on the dirt road. Zak sits next to me, brushing my arm with his own.

"Can I ask you about your dad?" Wow. I have no idea where that came from. I just don't want to think about Ariana being all buddy-buddy with him, and my uncontrollable tongue takes over.

"Why wouldn't you be able to?"

I shift, letting my legs fall, crossing them at the ankles. "Well, it's not your favorite subject."

"Uh…" He hesitates for like, three seconds before wrapping his arm around me again. "What do you want to know?"

I snuggle into his armpit, breathing in and trying not to be so obvious about it. But a moan slips out, and I snuggle farther into him to hide my face. "Like, has he tried to talk to you since that night?"

He shifts and I have to adjust so I don't fall flat on my face. His ears burn as his hand pulls my waist back to where it was.

"Yeah, he has."

"Do you want to talk about it?"

His mouth turns up in a sort of smile. "I talked to Ariana about it—"

"Oh." Yeah, I totally snap at him. That name sets my jealous teeth on edge.

"I was *going* to say… I talked to her, but you… you know how it is, you know? 'Cause you were there the first time around."

I nod and the fire in my stomach starts to fade. Zak wipes his palm on his jeans before he reaches for my hand to play with my fingers.

"H-he came by my house."

Oh shit. "What?"

"Yeah. Surprised the hell out of me."

"When?"

He takes a deep breath. "Right after, uh, our second driving lesson."

I shake off the discomfort crawling on my skin. That day sucked butt. I can't believe how much worse it was for him. First dealing with me then having his prick father show up. Oh gosh. While he was talking to his dad I was deciding who to give access to "downstairs" Zoe.

"Um, so what happened?"

He tenses and I lean up to look in his dark eyes. His mouth twitches, and he takes another deep breath.

"Nothing really. I didn't let him stay long." He drops his gaze, and I scrunch my lips together.

"You're lying. What happened?"

His cheeks blow up in mockery of me, and I pinch them together. Chuckling, he tucks me back into his side, hand trembling on my waist.

"He told me he was getting remarried, and he wanted to give us a heads up." Zak pauses, and I toy with the zipper on his jacket. "I don't know why. It's not like he let us know anything before."

His face goes a little red and I nod, unable to sort out what's going through my mind and what's actually happening. Zak's dad is getting remarried. Holy starships! This is huge! And he didn't say anything to me. Nada. Nil.

But he told Ariana.

Because *she's* a good friend. Not ashamed of herself even though crap about her flies around school just as much as it does about Zak. Zit Face, Dragon Virgin, and a few names I'm not even gonna repeat in my head. And she's not embarrassed to be seen with Zak in public, or to be with anyone from the D&D table.

Why can't I be like that? Then Zak may have confided in me.

"Are you okay? I know that's a stupid question but…" I stop, gauging his reaction. He's almost laughing at me. A real smirk on his face, eyes not teary but sparkly. He pulls me in for a hug—well, a tighter hug—and kisses the top of my head before answering.

"I told you, I really am okay." The vibrations from his voice rumble through my body, making me shiver. His hold tightens. "When he left, I always wondered if he'd ever try to come back. Weasel his way into my mom's heart again and then shatter it. But he didn't want that."

My whole body freezes, remembering exactly what Zak had said to me last night. The comparison to his father, how we both want to be back in his life. But as he voices his relief that his dad is moving on, I can't help but feel he doesn't want me back. He'd rather I move on as well.

"Now I have some sort of closure."

I nod, the rest of my body too frozen to move.

"Zo?"

"Um, yeah?" Oh crap, my voice is all crackled like I've been crying, and when I touch my face stupid tears are all over my cheeks.

"Hey." He grabs my shoulders and pushes me back, examining my wet eyes. "What's wrong?"

This is totally backwards. Zak's handling everything all mature and crap, and I'm the one blubbering like a fool.

"It's just…" I pause waiting to see whether my word vomit will push the frog out of my throat. It does. "You seem okay with him leaving this time, like you want it to happen. That your life is better without him."

Zak nods, eyebrows pulled together, probably wondering why this upsets me.

"This morning, you said me and your dad were both trying to… weasel our way back into your life."

I actually see the light click on behind his eyes. Pulling me in again, he squeezes me so tight I envision all the tears and snot propel from all the holes in my face.

"Oh crap, Zo, that's not what I meant. I hate myself for comparing you to him. I've regretted it since it came out."

"So, you don't think that?" I say into his shoulder.

"Not completely. I was upset and confused as hell. I've been trying to let you go because you're so different than the girl I used to know. But then you are that girl sometimes, even if it's just for a second, and I can't help all the… feelings I have for you."

He's being honest, but it doesn't make me feel any better. What if I'm not strong enough? If I let my weaknesses get the best of me? Let all the stares and the whispering trump my friendship with him?

"Maybe you're better off without me in your life too." Crap, it seems my mouth rules over my mind when he's around. I pull away, folding my arms across my chest and wiping the tears from my cheeks. "I don't want to put you through everything again."

"Are you expecting to?" he asks, tears brimming in his eyes.

I shake my head furiously. "No. No. I don't ever want to hurt you again. But Zak, I'm not perfect. What if I disappoint you? What if I fall short?"

"You're trying aren't you? I mean, that's what this is right?"

I nod, but I can't look at him.

"Please Zo," he says reaching for me. "I can't... I don't *want* to lose both of you."

"I don't want to hurt you," I whisper as he tucks his hand around my waist and pulls me into his side. "Not again."

"I don't want that either."

The sorrow in his voice pushes me on his lap—it just happens. Can't help it, because I can totally tell I'm hurting him right now. He seems somewhat surprised at my actions, but allows it. Taking a deep breath, I pull his head to lean against my shoulder and hug him so tightly I probably pop his eyeballs out. His breath hitches against my neck and a tear splashes the exposed skin on my chest.

He's crying.

Oh crap. I was hoping one of us would hold it together. But darn it all, that's not happening. I try to get the tears off my face while he holds me close and sobs into my shoulder. I stroke his hair, hoping I'm doing this right.

How did this happen? One second we're laughing and smearing sauce on each other and the next...

I tug his hair, pulling him back so he'll look at me. Attempting a smile, I wipe the tears from his cheeks and keep my hands there.

"Zak, I am sorry. About everything. With me. With your dad. I want to be here for you." I press my forehead against his, keeping my eyes locked on those dark irises. "I promise. I won't leave you alone again."

And I mean it. I never want him to go through anything alone. His hand moves from my back, and he cups my neck, pulling me to his face.

"Ahem."

My sigh is so loud, it's nearly a growl as Ariana clacks her tongue behind us. Zak chuckles and pulls me close to whisper in my ear.

"We'll finish this later."

Chapter 23

Where did all these sympathetic feelings came from?

Zak helps me off him, my face going red as I look at Ariana. She's got the you-killed-my-puppy look, but she's glaring at him, not me.

"I didn't mean to interrupt."

Yeah right.

"Are you ready to go get those keys?" She's still looking at Zak, and then it dawns on me. Is he leaving me here? To go with her? To get *my* extra key?

Zak nods and turns to face me, back turned at Ariana. I want to shoot her a "ha ha, you lose" sneer. But I hold it in as I look in his dark, dark eyes. Drool.

"I'll keep an eye on your car, 'kay?"

"What?!" Both Ariana and I say at the same time. Zak throws his hands up like we've got a gun to his head.

"Well," he stutters as he explains. "Zo, since the keys are in your house, you have to go get them. And since Ariana probably doesn't want to sit here alone in the mountains, I think I should be the one who stays."

He's totally right and both of us know it. But that doesn't mean we're happy about it.

"Fine. Get in the car." Ariana stomps around the truck and hops in, her glare never leaving my face. My lips curl in an evil smile, and I throw my arms around Zak, and plant a kiss right below his earlobe. She flips me off and I chuckle.

"What's funny?" Zak pulls back, his whole face red as he touches the spot I kissed.

"Nothing. I'll see you in a few."

He gulps, bouncing on the balls of his feet and looking at the top of my head.

Oh just go for it, Zak.

I take a step toward him, and he lets out a cute nervous laugh before giving me a kiss on my forehead.

Instant goose bumps. I rub them out as he opens the truck door for me. The second my butt hits the seat, Ariana revs the engine and Zak has to hurry and close the door before she takes off down the bumpy road. I snap my seatbelt on, watching her shift as easily as Zak does.

"Where did you learn how to drive?" My voice bounces around with my body as she plows the truck across the dirt.

"Sorry, I don't want to be in your presence for long." She shifts again when we hit the smooth gravel and speeds down the mountain pass.

"I wasn't talking about the *way* you're driving. I meant where did you learn how to drive stick?"

"Same place you did."

Jealousy crawls all over my body, igniting my face in what I imagine to be a bright shade of green. "Zak taught you?"

"Duh. That's what I said."

"How long ago?" What I really want to know is how long they've been so tight. I have no right to feel like she's moving in my turf, since I totally abandoned Zak, but that's exactly how I feel.

"Can we not talk?"

I fold my arms and press farther into the seat. "Fine. I'll ask Zak when we get back."

"Why do you care?" She shifts and throws me a nasty look. I knew she wouldn't resist the bait. "He's not yours to claim."

"He's not yours either," I shoot back.

Her voice rises. "You need to leave him the hell alone. I'm *not* saying that because I want him to myself—"

"Yeah. Okay," I say, rolling my eyes.

"I'm not! Not everyone is as selfish as you are. He's going through a lot right now, and he doesn't need a bitch like you hurting him. And that's exactly what you'll do. This is all a big game to you. Like you're bored and he's the only guy you haven't nailed so you take advantage of it. Of him. I'm tired of seeing him upset because of the shit you pull. You're going to make him think he has a chance, then drop him as soon as he pulls out his deck of magic cards, or asks you to go to Comic-Con with him. Or even if he even speaks to you in the hall."

She stops and catches her breath. I take it all in, knowing she has every reason to think these things. Still, I'm defensive and hurt. I'm ready to throw crap back at her, but I can't think of any.

"What? No comment?" She says it so forcefully spit flies onto the steering wheel.

"I'm not playing a game," I say through my teeth, looking out the window. "I'm trying to be his friend."

"Yeah right."

"I'm not! And don't try and tell me there isn't a tiny piece of you that wants me to leave him alone because you want him to yourself. It's obvious you like him."

"Yeah. I do."

My head whips around so fast, I kink my neck. I really didn't expect her to admit it.

"Why are you surprised? You said it was obvious." She starts to pick at a scab on her face from a popped zit. I'm amazed she can do that while she's driving.

"Does he know you like him?"

She barks out a laugh, putting her hand back on the gearbox. "Yes. But he's still stuck on you from forever ago. Don't ask me why. I don't put him as someone who's so shallow he just wants you for your skinny ass. Must be your *amazing* personality." She tosses her eyes at the ceiling and shakes her head. "Guys are so stupid."

I flinch like she's slapped me across the face. "He's stupid for liking me?"

"That's what I said, wasn't it?" She starts picking her face again. "You're going to leave him all broken and shit. And I'm going to be the one cleaning it up, like I have been for the past two years." Her voice changes, gets lower and hitches in all the right places to make me feel guilty. "Falling for someone who's in love with his whore of a neighbor isn't something I want to do over and over again."

How the hell do I respond to this? I'm hurt and pissed, but the sadness in her tone catches me off guard. And I try not to think about what she's going through, but I can't help it. Liking someone who not only doesn't like you back, but likes someone who's totally treated him like dirt. Someone who shoved him aside like he didn't mean anything. Ignored him, teased him, flirted with him only to send him cascading back into the same cycle. Then being the one he goes to for comfort. Rubbing his back and consoling him, not getting anything in return other than "you're a good friend."

"Hurry up." Ariana pulls in my driveway and puts the truck in what I think is neutral.

I nod, not able to speak. I'm not even able to hate her for hating me. Because I kind of hate me too.

Chapter 24

Dad's lap works as a confessional booth.

Hopin4lovin: How you feelin' drinky? ;)

    Zoester: Sore. You?

    Hopin4lovin: Like shit. I know we had plans to hang, but can we come over tomorrow?

    Zoester: haha, I totally spaced. I wasn't home tonight anyway.

    Hopin4lovin: Where were you?

    Zoester: On a date.

    Hopin4lovin: WHAT?? With who?

    Zoester: ;)

    Hopin4lovin: Oh! Did you slap some sense into that boy of yours? How did it go????

    Zoester: AH-MAZ-ING!

    Hopin4lovin: ?????

    Hopin4lovin: Come on! You have to tell me who he is.

    Zoester: nope. ;)

    Hopin4lovin: Why not? You make him up? lol.

    Zoester: NO! :) I'm not sure I wanna tell people, you know?

We haven't had the talk yet.

Hopin4lovin: well, have it soon. You're killing me!

...

...

Hopin4lovin: You still there?

Zoester: Yeah, sorry. Just thinking.

Hopin4lovin: ?

Zoester: Do u remember me from middle school?

Hopin4lovin: What are you talking about?

Zoester: Like, do you remember what I was like?

Hopin4lovin: I dunno. You hung out with your loser neighbor, I know that. Why?

Zoester: Say I was into that dorky stuff. Would u still hang out with me?

Hopin4lovin: LOL. R U kidding? What did u drink last night & is it makin' u crazy?

Zoester: Yeah, I guess. :)

Hopin4lovin: Look girl, you know I got your back no matter what. You're too cool to de-friend.

Zoester: You mean that?

Hopin4lovin: OF COURSE! Now knock it off! I gotta run, but ttyl?

Zoester: yup.

Hopin4lovin: good luck with your boy toy :)

I click off my browser and stick my laptop back under my bed. I had to talk to Hope so I could feel some normalcy. Like maybe I'm not as bad as Ariana thinks.

Yeah, it didn't work.

When we got back to my car, I didn't say much to Zak. I really tried to be upbeat and not let the conversation with his gal pal get to me, but I'm sure he could tell something was bugging me. He hugged me on the porch, and I went inside before I lost my mind and kissed him again. I don't deserve to touch him or be like that with him until I can freaking get my head on straight.

So I've had a lot of time to think. Like way too much time. My brain feels like mush now. And I'm anxious for Dad to get home. After talking with Zak and all the thinking, I want to give my dad a big hug and thank him for not ever running out on his girls.

I feel like I'm about to puke out my thundering heart when I see the headlights in the driveway. Don't know why I'm nervous. I mean, it's just Dad, but I haven't been the uber sweet Daddy's Girl so that may have something to do with it.

I hop downstairs, and when I hear the door click, I jump over to greet him.

"Hey Dad."

"Uh, hi." He sounds tired, and I don't blame him. I think today was a twelve hour shift.

"How was work?" I ask, taking his coat and hanging it up. His brow creases as he watches me, but he otherwise doesn't acknowledge my sudden interest.

"Long."

He plops down on the couch, stretching his limbs and rubbing his eyes. I really do feel bad for him. He works such long hours all the time. I take a deep breath before sitting down next to him. Tucking under his arm, I rest there, squeezing him around his large middle.

Either he's too tired or too stunned to react right away. But eventually he squeezes back and nestles his scruffy face against the top of my head.

"Thanks sweetie. I needed a hug."

I nod, and hold back all the tears building behind my eyes. He doesn't even know how much *I* need a hug from *him* right now.

"Now, what do you want?" His smile tugs my hair as it attaches to his whiskers.

I chuckle. "Nothing. I wanted a hug."

He laughs, and I jiggle around on his belly. "Really?"

"Is it that hard to believe?"

He laughs again. "Well, you have me a little worried." He squeezes my shoulders. "Is something bothering you?"

Yes. No. Kind of. My head's too mushy to think anymore and the Advil is wearing off. I want my daddy to hold me and tell me everything is gonna be okay, even though I'm pretty messed up.

"Dad?"

"Yeah?"

"Do you… like do you ever feel like people look at you differently? 'Cause of your job?"

He shifts, and I move with him so he can look me in the face.

"You mean, because I'm a welder and I don't work in the office?"

I nod.

"You know, I used to worry about that. But I don't anymore."

"Why not?"

He smiles and tucks me back around his stomach. "Because I'm good at what I do. And no matter how little money I get for it, it's enough to give my girls what they need. That's all that matters to me."

We sit there in silence for a few minutes before he says something.

"Why so curious?"

I shrug.

"Zoe…"

My gulp gets stuck in my throat, and I start choking. Dad gives me one good smack on the back, allowing me to clear the airway of my spit.

"It can't be that bad." He laughs again, but his face falls when he finally sees my expression. "What is it, sweetie?"

My eyes swim with tears, and Dad's face gets crazy with worry. "What happened?"

"Nothing happened. I'm, I don't know, confused I guess."

"About?"

I gulp again, this time it goes down the right pipe. "Dad, do you ever wish you were someone else? Like you could change your personality?"

"Why would you want to be someone you're not? Are people… are they making fun of you at school?"

"No. I… I don't want them to."

"Why would they? From what I've noticed, you're rather popular." He lightly chuckles, and gestures to my cell sitting on the couch. "That phone gets a lot of attention. More than it did a few years ago."

Yeesh. I'm so popular even my parents who work all the time know it? I shrug again. "I guess that's not really me."

His face goes the color of grape juice. "What do you mean?"

"I think… I miss who I really am."

"Who have you been, if not you?"

Oh gosh. Maybe I shouldn't have spilled so much. I don't know how to stop either, and next thing I know, I'm telling him everything. All the things people called me in middle school. Crying myself to sleep. Wanting to be accepted and popular. What I did to get that way. I almost spill about Cody, but I keep that in. I'm sure Dad would freak. After each new confession, a torrent of apologies escape through the tsunami of tears and snot.

"Dad, I'm afraid this is who I'm really becoming, and I don't want that. But how can I be myself without getting made fun of for it?"

He lets me fall onto his stomach and soak his shirt. I'm not sure if he's returned to his normal color yet, or if he's pissed or anything because he's so quiet. We sit there for a long time. He occasionally rubs my back and that sends fresh waves out my eyes. Like, I'm so crazy lucky to have a dad who cares, who listens, who works freakish hours for his family, and I cry my eyes out over that alone.

"Zoe?"

I sniff. "Um, yeah?"

He takes a deep breath while I wipe my flooded face with the back of my hand, but it's not doing much good.

"I wish I was around more. You know, spend more time with

you girls. But I can't. I'm sorry you've been dealing with this on your own."

I hear my breath catch as I see the water rise in his eyes. Oh no. He's going to cry. I *hate* when he cries. I have to stop this. Make it better somehow.

"Dad. It's not your fault," I repeat. "I've made a lot of mistakes, and I promise, I'm trying to make it better." And I mean it. I don't ever want him to feel he's the reason for me being so fake all the time. Because he's so not. He wasn't the one throwing food at me whenever I read comics at my lunch table. He didn't gossip behind my back, saying I had some sort of incurable nerdy disease that will make me a lifelong virgin. He didn't force me to sit in the back of the classroom so no one would stick gum in my hair. This is NOT HIS FAULT.

He seems to be thinking. And whatever goes through his head takes a long time to figure out. The silence in the room reminds me of that Star Wars scene when Obi-Wan has to sit there and watch as Darth Maul slices through Qui-Gon Jinn. I gotta sit here and await my own death sentence, because I *know* it's coming. I'll really be grounded this time, and probably for the rest of my teenage life. I think I blow up my cheeks and let the air out about fifty times before he finally says something.

"Zoe, no matter what you do, or who you are, there will always be people who don't understand." He picks up my chin and gives me an awkward smile. "Are *you* happy with yourself?"

Wow, not what I expected. And it takes me a minute to figure out which *me* he's asking about. I guess the answer is the same either way, and if my head wasn't so foggy, I'd go through the pros and cons list of Popular Zoe vs. Geek Zoe.

"Sometimes." It's about as honest as I can be.

He sighs, slowly returning to his normal color. "Then erase the part that makes you unhappy."

Is it really that easy? If I'm happy with myself then it won't matter what other people think? I'm not so sure, since I *was* myself in middle school, and it still hurt. But now that I think about it, no matter how many times I was teased, shoved, made fun of… I had things to make me happy. My books, my video games, my best friend. I had the very best of best friends and look what I did to him. Now when I see myself, I thought this was supposed to be better. Erase the teasing, but what do I have to show for it? Nothing, really.

Nothing that makes me happy.

"Hey, could someone give me a hand?" Mom asks as she walks through the door. She turns around and her eyes fall on me and Dad. "Oh!" She blinks a million times, like she can't decide whether or not she's dreaming.

I look at Dad and stifle a giggle. He rubs my back and says, "Why don't you go to bed. I'll help your mother."

"Okay." I give him another huge hug and make my way to my room. It's weird to be relieved and frightened at the same time. Like I'm glad I talked to someone about everything, but it doesn't make things better or worse. Just unknown, which scares the crap out of me.

Chapter 25

If only girl's night consisted of playing

Star Trek Trivia

"So, he let you off the hook?" Keira sticks the toe separator on my foot and grabs the nail file.

"Yup."

"Wow," Hope says as she flips through whatever she's reading on her iPad. "Ron would *never* let me hear the end of it if I told him about the party. What kind of magic potion did you feed your dad?"

Hope calls her parents by their first names, saying it helps her feel more adult. I have no idea where she gets this logic, since my parents still call their parents Mom and Dad, and they're about as adult as you can get.

Keira chuckles on the floor as she shakes up the Midnight Fury nail polish I picked out. "Magic potion? Hope, are you like four years old? Or are you turning into one of those acne-covered Luke Jaywalker obsessed freaks?"

"Skywa-" *Holy Jedi's, Zoe. Shut up!*

"What was that?" Keira asks, eyebrow raised.

"Nothing."

Hope clears her throat and puts her iPad on sleep. "Okay, then if not a magic potion…" she gives Keira fake glare, "then what happened?"

"She probably used her manipulative charm on Pops. Am I right?"

Not intentionally, no. Even if he hadn't come to my room twenty minutes after our conversation and told me he wasn't mad, I would've been completely happy with how things went yesterday. I was actually surprised he didn't put me on lockdown after all the spewage. He told me he was proud of who I am, as long as I'm proud of it. Not sure what he meant by that, but I don't think it was some pile of crap advice a parent feels like they should say to their kid. He sounded pretty sincere.

Only downside to this whole "confess my fake identity to my dad" thing, was I knew he'd tell Mom. And when she found out, first thing she did was come into my room with a pack of birth control.

Of course my first reaction was *What the hell?!* I tried explaining to her out of all the stuff I've done to make myself popular, having sex was not one of them. Dodged that bullet, thanks to Levi being a better guy than I thought. I should high-five him for that. She insisted anyway, and now I've got some Ortho-whats-a-ma-call-it on my nightstand.

Okay, I really don't think my dad expected me to invite my friends over, but I promised them I would, so here they are. I've been dying to hang out with Hope since the party so I could swoon over Zak, and I was really hoping Keira had plans with one of her three boy toys today, but obviously, she didn't since she's painting my toenails. I love the girl time, but I kind of wish these girls would be totally up for some nerdy video games or trivia. That stuff would totally ease my head about everything that happened this weekend.

Still, it feels good to have them *want* to be with me, even though by this time tomorrow, I'm pretty sure one of them won't be talking to me anymore.

That's right. Tomorrow, Geek Zoe will be going to school. She's going to pay attention in class, wear something that covers her body, and—gulp—sit at the D&D table and whoop all those wannabe players.

And if she can, give Zak a big Aragorn-and-Arwin-style whopper on the lips in front of everyone.

"All I did was give him a hug, and we talked for a bit last night."

Keira taps her nose with her pinky, careful not to swipe nail polish on her face. "See! Manipulative charm!"

I roll my eyes up toward Hope on the bed who giggles.

"Maybe Sierra can take a page from your book. Her ass is still grounded, right?"

I nod and flick my gaze to the door. Sierra's been poutier lately. Like *way* more than usual. I don't get it, and I kind of want to ask her what her deal is, but I don't want to start another argument.

"Oh I bet her boyfriend is going ca-ray-zee!"

Keira nods, her eyes way wide as she continues to paint my toes.

"Why do you say that?" I ask Hope, leaning my head up against the edge of the bed so I can see her face.

"Gosh girl, didn't you know? Sierra was totally going to give

Kevin her V-card the morning she stole your car."

Ack! "What?!" I move so quickly, Keira paints a huge blue streak across my big toe. "How do you guys know this? She doesn't even go to our school."

"Kevin does," Keira says, like it's the most obvious thing in the freaking world. She pulls out the remover and starts wiping my toe. "He had about fifteen condoms in his pocket." Both her and Hope laugh up a storm while I'm still trying to process. "I think they were going for an all day sort of thing!"

I try to giggle, but all that comes out is a small "heh". Sierra. My little sister planning on having sex. And Mom thinks *I'm* the one who needs birth control? Oh geez.

You know what totally sucks about this? Besides the fact I'm a total airhead and find out through my best friends instead of guessing the obvious, I can't help feeling if I was a better example to her… or if I let her know I'm really Geek Zoe deep down, she wouldn't be trying so hard to one up me.

"Oh! Oh! Oh!" Hope's sudden squeals pull me back into coherency.

"Oh my gosh, what?" I laugh.

"Speaking of boyfriends…" She winks and my face instantly fills with heat. IM-ing about Zak is one thing, but now I'm all nervous. I haven't even had the chance to give myself the pep talk, which I'm fully expecting to do tomorrow morning before school.

"What?!" Keira says by my feet before smacking my calf. "You have some fresh meat in your pocket and you haven't told me! Dirty ho."

"He's not my boyfriend," I correct them. Because Zak isn't, even though I *so* want him to be.

"Just letting him open your box?"

She did not just say that. "No, Keira. This is, like the real damn thing."

"What can be more real than that?" She shakes her head laughing before she blows on my toes.

Hope is way more sensitive. "Gosh Zoe, you serious? That's. So. Cute! It's not Levi is it?"

I shake my head and smile. "Nope."

"That's a shame," Keira says. "He's hella hot."

Ditto to half of that. He's super fine, but it's not a shame. Zak is way sexier.

"Yeah, but we're just friends."

"Does he know that?" Hope slides down next to me on the floor. "Because you two seem pretty close for just friends."

Yikes! Looks like I need to do some damage control. I don't want to give Levi or anyone else that impression. Levi was pretty touchy feely at the party even after he rejected me, but he may have just been keeping me from falling over. And Zak hugs Ariana, but whenever I see that happening it makes me want to hack a loogie in their direction.

"I'll make sure he knows."

"Make sure he knows I'm available when you tell him." Keira pulls the toe separators out and smiles. "I'm totally willing to dump one of the backups to make room for him."

I wiggle my toes and laugh. Keira may be a complete stuck up piece of work, but at least she's totally honest about herself. Maybe that's why I find it addicting to be around her. That and I crave her acceptance. Once she thinks you're cool enough to hang out with, no one else questions your social standing.

Too bad she'll be the first one to call me a "Jaywalker Freak" tomorrow.

Hope nudges me and gives me a pout. "Are you really not gonna tell us who he is?"

If it was just me and her, I may have spilled the nerdy beans. But Keira's here, and since magic potion got Hope an insult, I'm pretty sure having the hots for the dorkiest kid in school will get me much worse.

Crap. Damn it all to freaking loserish hell! Insecurities are going to win, aren't they? Will I ever find the guts to be myself one-hundred percent? I mean, if I can't even tell my friends, how am I supposed to face the entire student body?

I take a deep breath as my eyes dart to the floor.

"Maybe tomorrow."

Chapter 26

Epic fail, Geek Zoe.

A pair of jeans vs. a skirt so short, it screams, "You will reach the cooch in less than .25 seconds."

Put on the jeans, Zoe.

Low cut and skin tight pink top vs. form fitting T-shirt that may or may not have a Green Lantern Ring on the back that glows in the dark.

It's okay, Zoe. You can wear a jacket today to cover the full out "nerd sighting" affect this shirt will have.

Heels vs. flip flops.

Sweet! This decision is easy.

I blow up my cheeks and tuck my book against my chest. I do this weird in and out breathing thing, but since my cheeks are sort of blown, I sound like Darth Vader.

Badass! That helps actually. Darth Vader isn't afraid of anything. I can totally do this.

The air in my mouth flies out as I get downstairs to the kitchen. My face goes smack into a huge belly.

"Gah!"

Dad chuckles and gives me a quick hug before he pulls back. "Good morning!"

"What are you doing here?" I ask as I rub my nose. Dad's always at work by five o'clock sharp so he can be home at night. Which is a bunch of crock, since he's not home till like ten because he works freakish hours.

"I wanted to see you off." He parks his large body on top of the barstool and starts gobbling up his plate of hash browns and bacon.

I smile and grab a granola bar from the cupboard. "Short work day for you then?"

He pinches his lips together and doesn't look at me.

"Dad, please tell me you're not working till like three in the morning."

Another mouthful of hash browns gets shoved into his face before he looks at me. "I'll be home at one."

"Da—"

"It's okay, Zoester. I don't mind. I wanted to make sure you were okay before you went to school."

I do an emotional and mental checklist before answering. "Surprisingly, yeah." As long as I channel Darth Vader, I'll be fine.

He eyes me, doing that father thing when he questions whether or not I'm spouting off a bunch of phooey.

"Really, Dad." I laugh. "Don't worry." Because he shouldn't worry over this stuff. It's my problem and I'm going to deal with it.

I kiss him on the forehead—something else I haven't done in forever—and give him a small smile. "Get to work so you can come home sooner."

He chuckles and salutes me. "Yes ma'am."

Dad is such a dork. Maybe I take after him. I laugh and hop out the front door before he has any more chances to worry about me.

Today is also the first day I'm attempting to drive Manual Millennium all by myself. Though I totally think I can, I still glance over at Zak's house half hoping to see him outside so I can tell him to help me and half relieved he's not because I'm terrified out of my frakking mind.

Oh gosh. I better get to school before my dad comes out and catches me second guessing myself.

I stall the car five times. But not once in the school parking lot, so wahoo for that! There are a few people lingering by their cars, some guzzling RockStars trying to wake up before first period. My target person of interest is sitting by himself at the tables outside, with his Geometry book open, quickly trying to get his homework done by the looks of it.

Okay, Zoe I say to myself as I clear the crusts out from the corners of my eyes. *Be yourself. Don't think about what people are gonna say. Don't take anything to heart. Just be yourself.*

After a few Darth Vader breaths, I climb out of my car and walk over to him.

"Hey."

Levi scribbles down his last answer and slides his notebook in his text. "Hey." He starts tapping his mechanical pencil against the table, holding it like he would his drumstick. "How are you?"

"Good."

"Good."

He keeps tapping his pencil, and I clack my teeth in tune with it.

"Um, I wanted to, you know, say thanks for… well, for everything you did for me on Friday night."

The pencil stops. "No problem." He smirks and tucks an arm around my shoulder, pulling me down to sit next to him.

"I'm sorry. I shouldn't have pounced on you like that."

He shrugs. "It's okay. I could tell you weren't exactly being yourself."

"Yeah." I smile and try to be smooth about shaking his arm off me. "Did you mean what you said though? About being my friend?"

He laughs. "Yeah."

"You're okay with that?"

His eyebrow goes straight up. Damn boy and his resemblances to Zak. "What do you mean?"

"Like, you're okay with us being *just* friends, right?"

He laughs again. "Hells yeah. Why wouldn't I be?"

The biggest air of relief escapes my lungs. "Hope and Keira said something… never mind. I just wanted to make sure you felt the same way about where this, uh, is going."

"I told you already, I want to be your *friend*." He squeezes my shoulders and kisses the top of my head. Okay, hang on a second. Is this friend behavior?

"All right, but if we're buds, then we should probably tone down the touchy feely stuff." I elbow him in the ribs to keep up the playful banter, even though that's totally a contradiction to what I just said.

He nods and scoots about a foot and a half away from me, putting his hands up. "You got it. Hands off, I promise."

I roll my eyes and push him again. "Knock it off. You know what I mean."

"Yeah, yeah," he says with a grin. "I don't want to get in trouble with the boy you really want."

Whoa. "How—"

"I'm perceptive." He winks, putting his pencil in his mouth and picking up his book as he stands.

"You're not mad?"

He takes the pencil out of his mouth. "'Course not." He wiggles his finger between the two of us. "Friends, remember?"

Wow. This was a hecka lot easier than I thought it would be. Levi is pretty darn awesome. If I wasn't completely head over heels— I mean flip flops—crazy for Zak, I may have wanted something much more with this "pal" of mine. I wonder if he'll still want to be my friend once I start hanging out in Geek Town.

The bell rings and it's like fifteen thousand bricks fall into my stomach. Oh gosh. Here we go.

7:30. Nothing out of the ordinary, except I actually answer a few questions in class correctly. I get a few bizarre looks, but nothing else. Okay, I can do this.

9:00. I search like crazy for Zak in the halls, but I can't find him anywhere. Some girl asks if it was laundry day. I laugh it off and bolt to class.

9:10. Sweat like I'm standing in the middle of Mount Doom. I want to take my jacket off, but um, that's not happening. Make it out of the classroom fifteen pounds lighter.

10:45. Apply heavy doses of body spray in the bathroom while Hope tries to get me to show her what shirt I'm wearing. I escape seconds before she strips me down.

12:20. Still haven't seen Zak. He's not at the D&D table or anywhere else in the cafeteria that I can see. Argh! What. The. Hell?

I planned on the cafeteria being my big huge move. Like, "Look at me! I totally know how to play Dungeons and Dragons and I'm not afraid to show it!" Is it even worth it if Zak isn't here to witness me socially slit my wrists? Okay, awful image. But that's how it sort of feels if I'm being honest.

Wait a second. Why should it matter if he's here or not? I'm not doing this for him.

I'm doing this for *me*.

I pop the top of my water bottle and take a big swig. *Big Darth Vader breath, Zoe. Let's move in.*

Ignoring Keira and Hunter waving me over to join them at our designated table, I march straight to Dorky Heaven.

"Uh, hi."

You'd think I'd said something more obscene. Like "Wanna see my nips?" because that's how everyone stares at me.

One of the girls from fifth period seems to be the only one who can talk. She narrows her blue eyes and leans over the game board on the table. She's clutching her Monster Manual in the hand she points at me with. "Are you lost, Prom Queen?" Youch, her voice is so not nice at all. "I believe all the stuck up bitches sit over there." She nods to the table where Keira, Hunter, and now a whole bunch of other people from the popular crowd are gathered. And they're all staring at me like I've grown a tail out my butt. Keira seems to think it's one big joke, laughing her face off and whispering behind her hand in BJ's ear.

My cheeks are going to explode with how much air fills them. And my voice gets all shaky and cracked as I try to keep up the bravery. "I-I wondered if you guys had, you know, room for another player."

Dan, a boy from my seventh period class, chokes on the food he just stuck in his mouth. The girls sitting next to him pound on his back trying to clear his airway. His face is a little purple and his voice comes out a little strained when he answers me.

"D-do you even remember..." cough, hack, spit. *Gross.* He takes a sip of his drink, narrowing his eyes. "Do you remember how to play?"

I nod, ready to spout off all my stats, but Fifth Period cuts me off.

"Doesn't matter. You can't play with us."

Okay, I really didn't see this outcome. For some bizarre reason, I pictured them shocked but totally impressed. Not pissed off and intimidating.

Why is Zak not here? Would he tell them all to chill and let me join in? Or would he stand quietly in the background laughing at my humiliation.

No, Zak wouldn't ever do that.

He'd just make himself disappear.

The tears are coming. I can feel them prickle my eyes, and I gotta get out of here before they swarm my face.

"Okay, sorry."

I turn to leave, but Fifth Period isn't done talking to me.

"You get why, don't you?"

"Huh?"

"Why you can't play with us? You get it, right?"

No. Not really. But I don't want to talk about it either. I can already hear the belts of laughter from my "stuck up bitch" table and also some pretty confused chatter from the other cliques in the school.

I shake my head, forcing back the air I want to fill my face up with and also the tears that beg to come out my eyes.

She stares me down, gnawing the inside of her cheek before she says something. "We're not stupid. You mocking us or something? Because there's no way Miss High and Mighty would ever talk to us unless she was making our lives hell."

"I'm not mocking you." My voice is quiet because I'm done talking, and I want to be alone. "I really wanted to play, but it's no big deal."

"Bianca," Dan pipes up from the other end of the table. "Maybe we should let her. I mean, Zak and Ariana's spots are open."

That's a piece of news I'm interested about. But I can't ask because everyone else laughs at Dan's suggestion, reminding him of all the stuff I've done. Stuff I wasn't even aware of. How, yeah, I've made their lives at high school pretty darn hellish.

Shit, I have to get out of here stat.

No one even notices I'm leaving. Well, from that table.
Everyone else does though. I hear Keira shouting at me from across
the room, wondering what the hell I was doing. I try to ignore all the
other whispers followed by stunned silence as I walk by different
tables. It doesn't work so well. It's like I've been tied to a stake and
sentenced to burn.

I hightail it straight to the bathrooms. I know it's the most
cliché thing in the freaking world, but I. Do. Not. Care. I want to cry
it out before I get to last period.

And I do. Like, really let it out and I know I'm not even close to
being done when the bell rings. Curse Popular Zoe for skipping so
much class. If it wasn't for the pending doom of expulsion leering
over my head I'd go straight home.

Last period starts off with my ballsy move in the cafeteria and
my resulting bloodshot eyes as the main topic of discussion. I sit in
the back row praying to the Nerdy Gods to save me from this.

Mr. Sandstrom starts class and though it's quieter now, it
doesn't stop the note passing or the stifled giggles from the recipients.
I don't see the note, they conveniently left me out of the loop today,
but Ariana does. She doesn't laugh either. She crumples it up and
chucks it in her backpack. Not sure how to take that. She looks more
pissed off than usual, but it doesn't seem like she's pissed at me. Her
eyes are bloodshot too.

I bolt out the doors when the bell rings, ignoring Levi as he
chases me to the car.

"Hey," he says when he catches up, "are you okay?"

I nod and plaster a smile on so he'll let me go home. I don't want to be here anymore.

"Well, all right, but if you need someone to talk to—"

"Yeah, I know." I give him a quick hug. I can't talk to him about this stuff. I don't think he'll get it. Because he doesn't really know me, even though he thinks he does. "Thanks." Another fake smile and I hop in the car.

I stall another five times on the way home, and I don't even make it in the house before crying. I collapse on the porch and bawl my eyes out.

I've really screwed up everything. I should've never pretended to be someone I'm not because now I don't belong anywhere in school. The geeks hate me and the gods of high school think I'm a walking joke. And everyone else in between follows whatever crowd they want or shun everyone for being so judgmental. I don't fit in, and now I'm alone.

"Zo?"

Zak plops down on the porch and pulls me in his lap.

Well, maybe not as alone as I thought.

Chapter 27

Some nerdy medicine.

"You want to talk about it?"

We've been sitting on my porch for a good hour or two. Sierra came home and asked what the crap was wrong, but Zak waved her in the house as another flood came out my face. She listened, but came back with a bottle of water and tissues. I know it's stupid to think that meant something, but it did to me.

My eyes are pretty dry now, and I shrug from Zak's arms. He's looking me in the eyes, but suddenly my humiliation and hurt turn to anger at him for not being around, and I sock him square in the stomach.

"Oof!"

"Where in the effing Jedi's were you today Zakary Gibbons?!"

It takes him a minute to compose himself. "Sorry, Zo." He clutches his stomach and takes another breather. "I tried to catch you in the hall between classes, but I couldn't find you."

"And lunch?" I raise an eyebrow even though I know I can't do it right.

"I had to talk to Ariana." He quickly jumps into his explanation after I give him the evilest glare I can muster. "She had to know where I stood with her, because… well, I dunno what exactly is going on with…"

He stops and his face fills with what looks like red paint.

Oh my gosh.

"With us?"

More red paint fills his face. "Is that lame?"

I chuckle and curl back into him because I'm *so* not angry anymore. He's just so dang cute when he gets all embarrassed like that. "No. I had 'the talk'," I use my air quotes, "with Levi today too."

He nods and squeezes my shoulders. "Well, I'm sorry I wasn't at lunch. After I heard what happened, I felt like the crappiest friend 'cause I wasn't there for you."

I shrug. It's not his fault.

"I honestly didn't think you'd be waltzing up ready to play D&D." He laughs. "Oh man, I *wish* they would've let you play. You would've owned it."

He's trying to make me feel better, I can tell, but I don't feel better. In fact, I feel worse. Just a reminder of why they told me to leave them alone.

I get it now. I mean, the whole reason for my transformation in the first place was to escape all the people who made me feel like crap, like I wasn't worth anything because of the stuff I was into. It was a "keep your enemies closer" kind of thing. And then I became exactly who I hated, making fun of and ignoring all my old friends because I was embarrassed of who they are.

They all hate me now. But I'm not mad. They have every right to hate me.

"Zak?"

"Hmm?"

"Why don't *you* hate me?"

"What?"

I thought my eyes were dry, but they're not. Another wave of tears piles up behind them. "Why don't you hate me like everyone else does? I was even worse to you than I was to them, and you still... I mean, you're sitting here holding me. Why?"

He doesn't answer. He swipes away a single tear on my cheek with his forefinger and smirks, but still says nothing. Does he not have a reason? Or can he not find one?

"Why?" I ask again, blinking more tears out like crazy and shaking my head at my knees. "Why? Why? Why?" I slap my hands over my face and mumble into them. "I don't deserve it. You. Your friendship. Your—"

"Are your parents home?"

That's what he has to say? Where's Mr. Sensitivity?

"No. They're always working, you know that."

"Just wanted to be sure," he says as he stands. He extends his hand out to me.

"Where are we going?"

I set my hand in his and he pulls me up.

"I'm answering your question."

Now I'm the one who's not saying anything as he tugs me inside, straight up to my room. When we get there, he gently sits me on the bed.

Holy Obi Wan Kenobi, what is going through his brain? And please don't let him see the birth control on my nightstand.

He goes to my shelf, the carefully constructed one hiding all my nerdy literature. Smiling, he slides the door open and grabs the heavy X-Men book. Is he telepathic or something? Because how the hell did he know what was hidden on that shelf?

"What are you doing?" I ask, ready to slam my bedroom door shut.

"Slide over."

I do, still giving him the crazy confused and probably really stupid looking stare. He grins as he sits next to me, then tosses the comforter over our heads.

"Zak?"

The flashlight brightens his face before it lands on the book sitting between us.

"I know you think I didn't know," he says, flipping through the pages and opening it to the middle of the book where there is a collage of all the X-Men, "but sometimes, you forget to shut your blinds."

I'm only a little bit embarrassed, but mostly I can't help but be totally flushed because I'm under the blankets with him and his very sexy scent.

"Zo, I don't think I could ever hate you. You hurt me, but whenever I saw you grab one of those books and duck under here, I knew you were probably hurting too, and I'd let it go."

Whoa. "Just like that?"

He snickers. "I guess I make it sound easier than it was. But yeah, I'd let it go because I knew it wasn't the girl at school under this blanket. It was my friend." He grabs my hand and plays with my fingers. Yeah, I like that a lot. It makes my arm grow goose bumps. "Does that answer your question?"

I'm ready to kiss the crap out of him. This is the sweetest thing in the whole entire freaking world! But instead I sigh and nod. *He* doesn't hate me, which is amazing and more than I deserve, but everyone else wants me to run straight to the hell Popular Zoe originated from.

"What if I can't do this? What if I chicken out and go back to being the total bitch I've been since we started high school?"

"Do you plan on doing that?"

I shake my head, lifting my shoulders a tad. "I have no idea what to expect anymore."

It's getting a little uncomfortable under here. Not the conversation, that part is totally fine, but it's hot. I'm still wearing my jacket, but I don't know if I want to take it off. I've been successful at hiding the nerdy attire underneath it all day so far.

He takes in a huge breath and lets it out his mouth. My face gets covered with the smell of peppermint. It's super delicious. I wish I wasn't sweating a river.

"Why the X-Men?" he asks tugging the sleeve of my jacket. Okay, so now I know I'm obviously showing how hot I am. Or his super power is mind reading. Maybe he is telepathic.

"What?"

"Why this book?" He pulls the jacket off my shoulder, running his hand across my shoulder blades. I have to slurp back the drool piling in my mouth. "Why not the sisterhood of the what's-it pants book? Or The Notebook? Or a book at all? Why read *this* book?"

My jacket's off all the way now, and he runs the flashlight across my back, tracing patterns. I know he asked me something, but all I can think about it how amazing that feels.

"Zo?"

I shake my head clear and stare at the book. It's dark with the flashlight now being run around my back, but I've memorized the picture. Why do I like this?

"'Cause it's frakking awesome."

He chuckles. "Why?"

"Zak…"

"Humor me."

Gosh, I'd do anything for him right now. Even talk nerd with him.

"I dunno. I guess 'cause they are all totally hated for being different and still they fight to save the people who hate them, and that's pretty heroic." I pause before adding, "And they are all super badass!"

Zak barks out laughing, pausing the movement of the flashlight for a second. "Who's your favorite?"

"You know who my favorite is." I poke him in the chest. "You're wearing his shirt."

"Gambit?" he asks as he pulls the bottom of his shirt straight with his free hand.

"For real!" I flip to Gambit's page in the book. I can't see worth crap, but I know where it is. "I mean, look at him. Out of all the things he could use to charge and explode, he picks a deck of cards. I love it!"

"Hell yeah! That's why I like him too."

We keep laughing while he continues to play with my fingers with one hand and rubbing my back with the other.

"Why did you ask me that?" I ask after a few minutes.

"Well," he says, glancing behind me, "I wanted to let you know you can talk about this stuff with me. You don't have to hide it." The light clicks off, but it's not dark. My Green Lantern design on the back of my T-shirt lights up the space under the comforter. Is that what he was doing back there? Gosh, I'm so stupid. I should've picked up on that.

"How'd you know what shirt I had on?" I smile.

"I have the same one, silly girl."

Oh, that's right. I guess it's not the most subtle green. I slip my hands inside my sleeves and move the shirt around so I'm wearing it backwards, but it's brighter under the covers now.

"You don't think I'm a major dork for wearing this to school?"

He laughs and pulls me into his side. "I actually think it's way, uh, s-sexy."

Sexy? Did not expect that one. But then I think about him in his Gambit shirt, his blue plaid over it, his holey jeans and damn it, he's beyond sexy.

"Just wait till I start speaking Elvish."

He tucks my face between his palms and laughs. His eyes are so bright, something I haven't seen from him in a long time. Like he's super duper freaking happy. He's still chuckling when he says, "I've missed you."

Gah! He had to say that, didn't he? I lean in to kiss those darn beautiful lips, but stop myself. I've made this mistake twice before due to my horrible timing with this sort of thing. And it's…I mean it can't be right kissing him because I haven't proven anything. Only that I'm still that self-conscious girl who can't handle being made fun of. Even worse, I'm ready to go back to being the total popular beast because it's seems like the easy way out at this point.

Okay, so maybe that's not entirely true. Being popular isn't easy when you have to hide who you really are.

My eyes start filling up again, and Zak's mouth pops open.

"Hey, I-I didn't mean… I'm sorry if that was the wrong thing to say."

I shake my head. "It wasn't."

"Then why are you crying?"

Because I'm so messed up. Because I'm tired of hiding, but I'm afraid of losing everything and everyone if I'm myself. Because I've been a horrible person and I can't expect to change overnight. Because I want to kiss Zak but I can't make that mistake again. Because I feel horrible for making that mistake in the first place.

I toss the comforter off our heads and take a deep breath. "I'm sorry for kissing you." Yes, this is what comes out my mouth. And now on top of being a complete wreck, I'm embarrassed too.

"What?"

My cheeks blow up, and I shut my eyes tight. I let the air out in little wisps before answering him. "I don't know why I did."

His face puckers and his mouth opens, but either he doesn't know what to say or he's lost his voice because no sound comes out.

Gulp. "I guess I didn't know how to make you feel better. Or I was totally reading things wrong. I mean, I *know* I was, but I-I didn't like the way you were looking. Like, you were really hurt, and I wanted to take that away from you. But I went about it the wrong way, and I'm super super sorry. I wish I could take it back, or you'd forget it happened."

Oh man alive, would he say *something!* The silence is so much worse after I spew everything out there. Makes me feel like, yeah, he totally wishes I didn't—

"I don't."

"Huh?"

"I don't want to forget."

What is that pounding? Is it my heart beating a million light-years a freaking nano-second?

"Um, why not?"

He laughs and tosses his hands in the air. "Sweet Jedi's Zo, I had no *idea* how you felt about me until you kissed me. I was still under the impression I was only Dorky Driving Instructor to you."

"Really?"

"Well, yeah."

My head goes on rewind. I thought I'd been so transparent. "You really didn't see me get all flustered whenever you held my hand over the shifter? Or when you were in the shower with me? Or when you pulled that giant sliver out of my leg?"

His face gets redder and redder the more I spout off examples.

"I-I thought maybe you felt something… but then you called me a stalker, and I sort-of—"

"Sort-of what?"

"Believed you." He drops his eyes and starts picking at a hole in his jeans. "Zo, I've been thinking about you non-stop since that first kiss you gave me. Back when we were still friends and stuff. You remember?"

Hell yes I remember.

"Yeah."

"So when you called me a pathetic geeky stalker, I believed you."

Oh crap. That was so not one of my finer moments, and I still feel horrible about it. But what can I say to make it better? A weak ass apology doesn't seem to cut it anymore, but I'll give it a shot.

"Zak, I—"

"I know you're sorry, and you didn't really mean it. I know that *now*. Because you kissed me."

Whoa. Maybe I have better timing with the whole kissing thing than I thought.

"Okay, so why did you stop it?"

"You mean, why did I let you fall flat on your ass?"

I laugh and nudge him in the arm. "It didn't hurt that bad. I mean, the rejection hurt worse than the big bruise on my butt cheek."

He chuckles and keeps picking at that hole in his jeans. "You know why I stopped it. I was afraid of getting close to you, only to lose you again." He shakes his head. "That and you were still a little… groggy from that party."

Yikes! I hope he doesn't think I kissed him because I was still drunk or something.

"You gave me another chance, though. Why?" I shrug away from him and stand up, crossing my arms across my waist. "I still don't get it. So what if you saw me reading comic books under my blanket. It doesn't make up for all the crap I've pulled. Gosh, Zak, I'm a horrible person. Why the heck do you want to be my friend?"

He jumps off the bed and wraps his arms around me. Then he gulps like he reacted way too fast, so I cuddle into him, letting him know he's totally okay to hug me.

His chest relaxes under my cheek. "You will *always* be my friend." He tilts my face up, those darn black eyes pulling me under. "I know who you really are, and I like it. I wish you felt the same way about yourself."

I do think I'm pretty cool in the dorkiest way possible. It's everyone else who will think I'm lame to the umpteenth degree.

Except him. This guy standing here telling me he likes me for who I really am. Who called me sexy for wearing a Green Lantern shirt and talking X-Men under my comforter. Who's given me way more chances than I deserve to be the friend and person I know— and he knows—I can be. Butterflies don't even begin to describe what's going on in my stomach.

The goofiest of grins plasters on my lips. "So, you didn't stop kissing me because you don't feel *that* way about me, right?"

He chuckles. "Didn't you notice how flustered *I* got? How weak I am when it comes to you? Dammit, Zo, you've got me." He pauses, pressing his forehead against mine. I'm pretty sure I'm not breathing.

"If you want me."

How could I not want him? He's all I've wanted since forever.

I pull him into a tighter hug, kissing his earlobe before I whisper to him. "Nin ore lin."

He laughs and pulls back to peck me on the forehead.

"You have my heart too."

Chapter 28

Maybe she's not the devil.

It's two in the morning and I'm still wired. There's no way I'm getting any freaking sleep tonight.

Reason one: Dad's still not home even though he said he'd be. Darn father. At least he's texting me, which is super cute, by the way. His fingers are too big for the autocorrect so he sends some hilarious unintentional messages, but the last one he got right.

i'll be home soon sweetheart just washing up GO TO SLEEP

PS, he doesn't know how to use punctuation, but his caps lock works just fine. Maybe my dorkiness does come from my daddy.

Reason two: I keep playing the afternoon with drool-worthy potential boyfriend on repeat. Over and over and over. My back tingles from reliving the flashlight being dragged across it. I will wear a glow-in-the-dark shirt every day for the rest of my nerdy life if he does that every time I do.

And is it wrong for me to think he's so… perfect? I mean, that's usually off-putting, right? But he is so geeky perfect for me, it's not even funny. Why does no one else see this about him? I'm not complaining because that means I get him to myself, but really, what is wrong with the girls in my high school? It's a sad day when only Ariana can see how freaking hot and amazing the boy is.

Or maybe they all have a secret crush on him but are too afraid to tell anyone because of his reputation. Um, like me.

Reason three: I hate to admit it, but I'm effing terrified of going to school tomorrow… or I guess in a few hours now. I'm not sure who to hang out with, or how to act. On the one hand, tomorrow I have classes with Hope, and I'm sure she'd be totally cool with whatever. She did say she had my back no matter what. I really hope she meant that.

Then on the other hand I want to hang out with Zak and his friends. They really are more my group of people. But they'll all be shooting fiery arrows at me with their eyes.

And I know it's super lame to keep thinking this, but I don't want to be laughed at. Thinking about everyone's face when they see what I plan on wearing makes my heart stop beating for a few seconds.

Yeesh, can't think about that anymore. I'd rather think about kissing Zak again. I'm surprised he didn't kiss me earlier. We totally had the sexual tension thing going on, but I was too chicken to go for it and then get another rejection, despite all he was saying. And he never dove in. Whether that was because he was chicken too or he didn't want to is something I'll never know. But it makes me all the more self-conscious.

Something creaks outside my door and zaps me from all my jumbled thoughts. Oh good, Dad's home. It's about time.

I hop out of bed and slowly open the door.

Huh. The hallway by Mom and Dad's room is empty. Weird. "Hey."

I jump back with a "Holy Batman!" and trip over my rug on the floor, landing square on my already bruised butt.

"Sorry," Sierra says, stifling a laugh as she helps me back up, "I didn't mean to scare you. I thought you saw me."

"I thought Dad was home." I straighten my PJ top. "What are you doing awake?"

She shrugs. "Can't sleep."

"Me neither." If she didn't sound so sad, I probably would've told her to go back to bed. But I can't because despite our not-so-sisterly relationship, I still want to make sure she's okay. "Wanna talk about it?"

She shrugs again, but her eyes flick to mine, totally saying yes. I smile and climb under the sheets, patting the place next to me.

I can count the sister bonding moments I've had on one hand... on one finger actually. But still, she looks like she needs someone to talk to, and I'm wide awake anyway.

"What's up?" I ask as she slides in next to me.

She nibbles her bottom lip and looks at her fingers. "A-are you okay?"

"Huh?"

She sighs. "Zoe, you were crying for almost two hours out on the porch in our nerdy, yet *totally* sexy neighbor boy's arms. Forgive me if I'm a little worried."

"You're worried about me?" I know I sound like a friggin' idiot, but I'm in shock. The only time Sierra shows concern is when she wants something. And I had no idea she realized how super sexy Zak is.

"I've never seen you like that."

"I'm fine." I attempt a smile. "I didn't mean to scare you. It was a tough day at school."

"What happened?"

"Just utter humiliation." We both laugh, and I link elbows with her. "But thanks for making sure I was okay."

She nudges my shoulder, and we sit in silence for a minute. We hear Dad get home, but he goes straight to his room. The shower goes on, and I listen to the water run through the pipes, my eyes drooping.

I glance at Sierra to see if she's zonked out, but her cheeks are blown and her brow furrowed.

"Are *you* okay?"

She gives me a half smile. "Do you like him?"

"Who?"

"Zak?" She nods toward the window.

Majorly blushing right now. I'm glad it's so dark. "Uh, yeah. I do."

"And, you aren't worried about what that'll do to your rep?"

Now I blow up my cheeks and let the air seep out before I answer. "Not really anymore, no."

"Wow."

"What?"

"I… I mean I wish I could be that confident."

Yeah, me too.

"So you don't think less of me for liking the geeky next door neighbor?"

She shakes her head. "I'm actually way jealous."

What? "Why?"

"Because I'm pretty sure he won't pressure you into doing anything you don't want to do."

Her face flushes in the moonlight from the window. Oh gosh. Is she talking about her boyfriend?

"Um, I heard about you and Kevin."

Her eyes zap to mine, totally scared as hell. "Nothing happened. I mean I haven't slept with him."

"I know. Your butt has been grounded since the accident."

A huge sigh of relief escapes her. "Can I tell you something if you promise not to tell anyone?"

I nod, sliding closer to her.

"So, that morning… the morning I stole your car…"

"Yeah…?"

"I-I crashed on purpose."

"What?!"

"Shh!" Her eyes go to my door then land back on me.

"Why the heck would you do that, Sierra?"

She frowns. "I crashed on purpose because, well, I don't think I'm ready to…" Her voice trails off and her eyes land smack on my birth control.

"Have sex?"

She nods. "I'm sorry. I know you're probably even more pissed at me now, but I—"

"I'm not mad." Because I'm so not mad at all. "I'm kind of happy you crashed my car. Even if it was really stupid because you landed yourself in the freaking hospital! But, I'm not mad."

"What?"

"I'd rather have a folded engine than have you do something you're not ready for. Is it 'cause you felt like you had to in order to keep him as your boyfriend?"

"That and it's what people expect from me." She sighs. "You know how it is. You were my age too when you gave up the V."

I shake my head. "Wanna know a secret?"

She cocks her eyebrow. "O-kay."

I drop my voice and lean in, smiling. "I'm still a virgin."

"No way!"

"Way." I laugh and she laughs with me. I swear this is the most relaxed we've ever been with each other.

"Why does everyone think you aren't then? I mean, I thought with all the guys you've dated one of them was bound to get in your pants."

"That's the problem with my reputation. And the one you're trying to keep up too. Guys will think that, and some won't stop until they get what they want." *Ahem... perv boy, Cody.* "If you aren't ready, you need to make sure Kevin knows."

"What if he dumps me? Or calls me a prude? Or spreads nasty rumors about what a tease I am?" Her eyes water. "How... how do I handle that?"

I don't know how to answer, because I'm still trying to figure that out myself. But I can't just sit here either. I wrap my arm around her and squeeze her shoulders. If there is anything I can do, then I will. Take away all this pain and protect her from anything that'll hurt. Especially since she'll be entering the halls of high school next year. She shouldn't have to go through what I've gone through. The fake stuff, I mean. She should be proud of who she is, since she's pretty cool. I've never told her that. I probably should.

"No matter what happens, you won't be handling it alone. I promise."

Chapter 29

I think Zak is really Peter Parker

Thwump!

I shoot from my bed, looking for Sierra but she must've gotten up already. What time is it? And what the heck was that noise?

"You really need to start setting your alarm, silly girl." Zak climbs into the window, easily maneuvering to a crouched position, ducks under the frame and hops into my room. He lands in a Spiderman-like squat before straightening.

Holy hell, that was hot.

"Get your sleepy butt out of bed," he says, smirking at my messed up hair, "you owe me a ride to school."

I don't even look at the clock before standing up on the bed and leaping into his arms. He lets out an "Oof!" as I almost knock him on his ass.

"I owe you a ride, huh?" I ask, keeping my legs wrapped around his waist, but pulling back so I can see his wicked hot face. "How do you figure?"

He shifts my weight, but keeps a hold of me. His cheeks are super flushed and I get all giddy. It's so freaking awesome I can make him as crazy nervous as he makes me.

"I drove you to school when you didn't have a car, right?"

"Yes." I hop off him, though I really don't want to. I run my hands on the inside of his plaid overshirt. "What's wrong with your car?"

"Nothing. My mom had to take it today. Hers is at the shop."

He leans in, sending waves of peppermint in my face. Oh dude, he can't kiss me right now because I've got major morning breath. Didn't help I had a midnight snack of parmesan artisan chips either.

I take a step back, trying to be discreet about covering my mouth. "Well, wait downstairs Mr. Impatient."

After I shove him playfully out the door, I develop supersonic speed. I'm dressed and ready to go in less than five minutes.

"Another jacket?" Zak asks as I descend the stairs. I know it's like a thousand degrees outside, but I don't care.

"Baby steps." I wink, and he rolls his eyes.

Zak's a major gentleman, as always. Opens my door for me, holds my hand on the shifter, but only after he asks permission, and when we get to school, he warns me before we get out of the car he's not going to pressure me into anything I'm not comfortable with.

Normally, when a boy says this it means sex, but I know he means all the simple things. Holding hands, kissing, heck even talking to him before I'm ready.

I'm one helluva lucky girl.

"Zo?" Zak grabs my arm before I can get out of the car. "I'm about to say something that's going to sound egotistical and cocky, but I have to ask."

"Nice disclaimer." I laugh. "Go for it."

He takes a huge breath and doesn't look at me. "You sure about this?"

I raise my eyebrows and stifle a grin. "Um, sure about what?"

"This." He waves his hand between us. Oh gosh, is he asking what I think he's asking?

"Zak?"

"Sorry," he says to his lap, "I just know how it is."

Wait, huh? "What are you talking about?"

"I don't think I ever told you I understood why you did what you did. Why you changed. Because I get it. Trust me. Some days, it… hell, it sucks."

He's still talking to his lap and I'm gagging on my tongue. He always seemed so cool with how he's treated. I never thought about it hurting him at all because he never showed it. But being the target for everyone's insults is something I can definitely relate to.

"I know what you're giving up. And I have to make sure, is it only because of me?"

I still can't find my voice and when he looks up, I'm pretty sure my face looks super dumb.

"Sorry. I know it's stupid for me to think you'd be willing to risk social suicide for someone like me. Forget I asked."

"It's not stupid." I grab his hand and tuck my fingers between his. "You *were* the reason. At first."

He cocks his eyebrow, making me temporarily lose my train of thought. He's got to teach me how to do that. "Please tell me I'm not the reason now. I'd be a hypocritical shite if that's the case."

"How so?"

"Asking you to change yourself to impress me."

I laugh and squeeze his hand. "Zak, I'm totally jealous of you. You deal with people giving you crap every day, but you don't change yourself to please them. And you shouldn't have to either, because, well, you're frakking awesome." I pause while he sort of laughs. He's totally nervous, and it's not helping my nerves at all. How do I explain this?

"I kept asking myself why I couldn't do that. Ignore what people thought of me and be myself. You were... *are* the only person who knows who I really am and you like me for it. You make me, I dunno, proud to be a total dork.

"So, yeah, you're part of the reason still, but I'm not doing this just for you. I'm doing this for a lot of people. Myself included."

Mom and Dad, especially Dad. When I briefly peeked in his room to see if he was at work or sleeping still, I was happy to see him tucked in bed, snoring so loud I'm surprised the house hadn't crumbled into a million pieces. He's so awesome to do what he does for us. And he could totally get an office job if he wanted. He's smart and good with people, but he said he likes what he does even if it doesn't pay as much as he'd like it to or gets him the respect I freaking know he deserves. But even though I hardly ever see him, when I do, I can tell he's happy. I totally want that too.

Sierra. After talking to her last night and seeing the look on her face, she's so scared to go against the crowd. If anything I've got to prove to her that even though it's scary, it's worth it. But to be honest, I still have to prove that to myself.

Zak. Yes, he is still part of the reason. I've hurt the guy way too much, and he's my friend dang it. Hopefully way more than my friend. I'm freakishly and obsessively in love with him. I don't know if he's quite there with me yet, since I've metaphorically Force-choked him over the past couple years, but I don't care. I love him. So I shouldn't be ashamed of him anymore.

And me. Yes, I *have* to do this for me. Geek Zoe. Just like my dad said, there will always be people who don't understand who I am or what I choose to do with my life. But screw 'em. I totally get what I'm about to lose today when I walk through those doors. But unlike yesterday I won't let the whispers and the laughs get to me. If I get picked on, I better develop a tough skin. Like Ariana and Fifth Period Bianca. They don't take crap from anyone.

Besides, what I'm losing couldn't possibly add up to what I'm gaining. Like my dad said, erase the parts that make me unhappy. I guess that means emphasizing the parts that do. So that means Harry Potter, Doctor Who, Lord of the Rings, and all my comic book buddies need to know I'm not embarrassed of them either. Geek Zoe makes me happy.

Zak leans over and tucks a loose strand of hair behind my ear. Just like in Zombieland. I get giddy over it.

"You promise?"

I put my forehead against his. "I promise."

♡

7:30. I sit in the front of the class so I don't see the continued note passing from the cafeteria display yesterday. Apparently it's still a hot topic. That and "Zoe spotted in the same car as Dork Lord" flew around the school like the info was carried via Firebolt.

But sitting in the front helps. I try to think of what's in front of me rather than what's going on behind me.

9:10. I see Zak in the hallway, he's busting it to class. I wave and give him a quick hug, then bolt to my class. A few people see the display of affection, getting slack-jawed and wide-eyed. Nothing I can't handle. Besides, hugging Zak sends the "I'm totally in love with this guy" butterflies through my stomach instead of the "Oh my gosh, what if someone sees us?" butterflies. That's good, right? Progress…

10:45. Hope drags me into the bathroom between classes and begs me to tell her what is going on.

"Keira's saying you wanted to sit at the Nerd-O table yesterday at lunch. Then today you show up with King Dork Dax or whatever his name is. Are you feeling okay?"

I smile at my best friend, hoping she'll get it, and she's still got my back like she said.

"His name is Zak. And he's the guy I've been telling you about."

All the air rushes out her tiny frame, and she clutches the sink to keep from falling. "Oh. My. Hell."

"Are you okay?" I ask, stifling a laugh and holding her arm.

"What universe have I stumbled into?" she asks poking my face as if I'm some sort of apparition. "Who are you?"

"Knock it off." I grin and bat her hand away.

"I just… I can't believe it." She shakes her head, her eyes still way wide. "How long have you been banging your next door neighbor?"

"I'm not sleeping with him." I sigh, wishing this conversation would go better. Hope has always been so cool about everything, but now she's looking at me with shock and disgust. So not what I expected. "I just *really* like him."

"Oh my gosh. Is this what you were trying to talk to me about the other day on IM?" She sets her hands on my shoulders. "You want to commit social suicide for... for *him?*"

What is it with people saying I'm committing suicide here? Oh crap, maybe I can't... no, I have to do this. I have to stop being so damn self-conscious.

"I'm not doing it for him," I whisper. "Hope, do you seriously not remember who I was in middle school?"

She doesn't answer.

"Well, let's just say Head Dork wasn't Zak, it was me. And... I'm still into that stuff."

She starts prodding my face again. I shove her hand away.

"Are you serious?" she asks. "Or is this some bizarre not-so-funny joke you and Keira are trying to pull?"

I push back the tears starting to form behind my eyes. I get why she's acting like this, and at least she isn't laughing at me, but I wish she'd take me into a hug and tell me it doesn't matter to her. I can't help but feel I'm ending a friendship.

"It's not a joke. I'm sorry I haven't been totally honest with you about this, but you can see why I wasn't. There's no way in hell you would've ever been my friend if you knew I was a closet nerd."

242

I wait for her to argue, or to tell me something encouraging like, "You'll always be my peep. No worries!" But she doesn't. She doesn't say anything. I leave before I really start crying.

Now I know how it feels when your best friend is embarrassed by you.

Karma's a bitch.

Chapter 30

Apparently, I don't do things half-assed.

If the conversation with Hope hadn't happened, I probably would feel a little more confident right now.

Well, maybe not. Keira and Hunter are laughing while stealing glances in my direction. BJ ignores everything except Keira's exploding cleavage. Cody's at the other end of the cafeteria with some sophomore girl on his lap, head cocked as if to say, "Take a look at what you're missing!" Everyone else in the cafeteria looks at me standing in the doorway, some pointing and whispering to their friends while others just wait.

What is she gonna do today?

I'm looking for Zak. He's not at the D&D table, but Ariana is, so he's not with her. I wish there weren't so many people in my school. Almost all eyeballs are on me, but I can't seem to find those dark beauties in the crowd.

"Hey whore!" Keira giggles from across the cafeteria. "Get your ass over here before you get sucked into Loserville again."

The whole table laughs at Keira's "clever" insult while the D&D crowd rolls their eyes. Bianca gives me the look like, "don't you even think about coming over here again or I'll pummel your ass" and everyone else looks at me, waiting to see what I'll do.

This is what I see.

Popular Zoe, sitting with her group of friends in her skankiest dress code allowed skirt. The boys are all fawning over her while the girls ache to be her. Keira's getting greener by the second as Hunter glides his hands all over Popular Zoe, and she shows nothing but indifference. The things people say behind her back aren't true so they hurt less. They hurt... but less.

Geek Zoe, sitting at the D&D table totally zoned into the game. She makes a move that everyone goes "ooooh!" over. She's wearing her favorite Spiderman shirt and does a victory dance which makes people passing by totally make fun of her. But she lets it roll right off her because the other players are laughing and dancing too. This is how it'd be if Geek Zoe had beaten Popular Zoe down before high school started.

The biggest difference I see?

Someone who isn't me vs. someone who is.

I shake my head, trying to clear everything in it. When I open my eyes, I see him. Zak walks in the doors that lead to the bleachers and outside tables. He gives me a small smile when he catches my eyes, but doesn't move.

There are a million people between us. I can't make a straight line to his arms, but they aren't my destination right now anyway.

I march right up to a table in the center of the cafeteria. People are sitting at it, but I don't care. I climb on top and look at my audience, which is now half the student body. Everyone is telling their friends to look in my direction, some already laughing, but most are gaping at me.

My cheeks blow up, and I start doing Darth Vader breaths again. *Remind yourself why you're doing this Zoe! You're tired. You're so tired of being someone you're not. You're tired of being afraid. You're tired of everything. Just do it! Like a friggin' bandaid!*

I unzip my jacket and toss it on the floor. Here I stand in my bright blue Superman shirt.

"The Star Trek franchise includes six series: *The Original Series, The Animated Series, The Next Generation, Deep Space Nine, Voyager,* and *Enterprise,* totaling 726 episodes."

The cafeteria is dead silent and my heart is pumping in my throat, but I keep going.

"Tom Baker, who occupied the Tardis between 1974 and 1981, is the longest serving Doctor on Doctor Who. In *Harry Potter,* dragon's blood is an effective oven cleaner. Yoda is sixty-six centimeters tall, but still one of the most powerful Jedi's of all time."

My cheeks blow up as I cast my eyes around the room, spotting Levi near the pizza line, twirling his drumsticks. He's grinning at me, but it's not one of those grins like he's making fun of me. He's smiling like now he *gets* it. Why I was "lost." He rolls his drumstick in the air, telling me to keep going.

I look over at the D&D table and let all the air out of my cheeks. People are starting to laugh, but I ignore them.

"There's a seventy-five percent chance of a blink dog appearing behind you, based on a 12-sided die. The Oathblow whispers to its wielder in Elven. The main attack of the Demi-Lich is soul trapping, which is majorly badass! It's been a while since I played but I still know what STR, DEX, CON, INT, WIS, and CHA stand for."

I turn to Zak and smile. "I'm fluent in Tolkien's Elvish language... both of them. Though I prefer Sindarin over Quenya."

And with that, in true geeky fashion, I step down from the table, tripping over my feet and smashing face-first into someone's lunch tray. Everyone busts out laughing, and if my face wasn't covered in mashed potatoes and chocolate pudding, they would see how red it is.

So much for marching straight into Zak's arms and giving him the kiss I planned on giving him. He's standing right where he was during my nerd explosion. He's smiling... not laughing at me, but giving me that same smile he gave me yesterday when he said he missed me.

I really wish I wasn't covered in food.

Then without hesitation at all, he grabs a tray and dumps it over his head. *He* marches to *me*, not wiping my face or anything before he plants a whopper of a kiss on my lips.

I know people are laughing at how gross this is, and some are probably stunned straight to hell at this more than disgusting public display.

You know what? I don't frakking care.

"That. Was. The. Sexiest. Thing. I've. Ever. Seen," he says between kisses. I'm smiling even though my lips are super busy right now. Gosh, he's so amazing. I don't care if everyone thinks I'm a friggin' nerd. I *am* a nerd, but I like it. I like this. All of it. All of him. And he likes me too.

We stand there and make-out while the cafeteria makes fun of us and tosses more food in our direction. But there's no way I can feel anything but happy right now. They're all just a bunch of people who don't understand.

And the people who do, I can hear them too. A few calls of "Way to go Zak!" and "Dude, that was awesome!" reach my ears through all the noise. And even if no one else understood, what the heck does it matter? I'm finally, *finally* being myself. All the way.

Zak pulls from my lips, taking his plaid shirt off and wiping my face. I wipe his at the same time.

He smiles that beautiful and perfect smile I don't ever want to see go away.

"Amin mela lle."

Holy Tardis. I just made a complete idiot of myself, ruined my popular reputation, and lost most of my friends. Maybe Hope will come around, I really hope she does. And maybe Zak's buds will forgive me at some point. The humiliation may be enough for them to say I got what was coming to me. And tonight when I get home, it won't be the food thrown at me or the whispers or insults that I'll remember. It'll be this moment, right here. Because none of that other stuff matters. Today has just become one of the best days of my freaking life.

I pull Zak's face toward mine, talking against his lips.

"I totally love you too."

Acknowledgments

Thank you Google, for confirming all my nerdy knowledge, and making me proud when I got it right.

Thank you reader, for getting to this page, and for sticking with Zak and Zoe and all their geekisms.

Thank you Potterheads, Whovians, Jedi Knights and Sith Lords, for collecting, reading, dressing up, posting inside fandom jokes, and basically being the most awesome people on earth. It's people like you who inspired me to write this.

Thank you Mommy, for showing off my books everywhere you go, for letting me talk your ear off about characters and funny moments, for always telling me to write down my ideas, and for telling me you're proud of me. You make me feel like the luckiest daughter in the world.

Thank you Becki, Jenny, and Jon-Jon for being nerdy siblings. And thank you Daddy, for watching Lord of the Rings every Saturday for about three years.

Thank you stick shifts, for making sexy men even sexier.

Thank you Makeready Designs and Meet Cute Photography for giving me the best cover makeover ever!

Thank you Hope Roberson, Jenny Morris, Kelley Lynn, Leigh Covington, Jade Hart, Suzi Retzlaff, Rachel Schieffelbein, Jennie Bennett, Jessica Salyer, and Lizzy Charles for being schweet critique partners, for loving Zak and Zoe, for leaving LOL's on my manuscript, and for being my friends. I love you guys more than a

Star Wars fan loves to quote Yoda.

Thank you Angie Cothran, Emily King, Ilima Todd, Jolene Perry, and Kyra Lennon for beta-ing this Nerdy baby of mine, and always being my support beams.

Thank you Peggy at Le' BookSquirrel, Kristin at I Heart Books, Anitra at Can't Read Just One, and Lauren Sweeney at Madison Says for lighting up my Facebook feed with my books, sharing my statuses, and basically being all around KICK BUTT book bloggers.

Thank you Theresa Paolo, for being my constant ear. For loving the story before you even read it. For taking this journey with me. Letting me IM you and email and call and text even if it's midnight your time, and knowing exactly what to say. I would never make it through a manuscript if it wasn't for you.

Thank you Harry Potter Scene It, for inspiring this story.

Thank you children, for telling Mommy to play Lego Star Wars and use it as research. I agree, kiddos.

And last, because I always save you for last… Thank you Joshy poo, for playing HALO on our first date, for quoting Ninja Turtles when you first held my hand, for saying you love me when we went and saw Harry Potter, for proposing with the ring box upside down, for wanting Han Solo and Princess Leia on top of our wedding cake, and for letting me keep a giant poster of Edward Cullen in the computer room. You are my nerdy love story.

About Cassie Mae

Cassie Mae is the author of a dozen or so books. Some of which became popular for their quirky titles, characters, and stories. She likes writing about nerds, geeks, the awkward, the fluffy, the short, the shy, the loud, the fun.

Since publishing her bestselling debut, Reasons I Fell for the Funny Fat Friend, she launched the FLIRT line at Random House and founded **CookieLynn Publishing Services**. She is represented by Sharon Pelletier at Dystel and Goderich Literary Management. She has a favorite of all her book babies, but no, she won't tell you what it is. (Mainly because it changes depending on the day.)

Along with writing, Cassie likes to binge watch Once Upon A Time and The Flash. She can quote Harry Potter lines quick as a whip. And she likes kissing her hubby, but only if his facial hair is trimmed. She also likes cheesecake to a very obsessive degree.

You can stalk, talk, or send pictures of Luke Bryan to her on her Facebook page: **https://www.facebook.com/cassiemaeauthor**

22910847R00156

Printed in Great Britain
by Amazon